RANGER'S REVENGE

RANGER'S REVENGE

Nelson C. Nye

Chivers Press • G.K. Hall & Co.
Bath, England   Waterville, Maine USA

This Large Print edition is published by Chivers Press, England, and by G.K. Hall & Co., USA.

Published in 2002 in the U.K. by arrangement with the author c/o Golden West Literary Agency.

Published in 2002 in the U.S. by arrangement with Golden West Literary Agency.

U.K. Hardcover   ISBN 0–7540–4756–3 (Chivers Large Print)
U.K. Softcover   ISBN 0–7540–4757–1 (Camden Large Print)
U.S. Softcover   ISBN 0–7838–9673–5 (Nightingale Series Edition)

The text of this Large Print edition is unabridged.
Other aspects of the book may vary from the original edition.

Set in 16 pt. New Times Roman.

Printed in Great Britain on acid-free paper.

British Library Cataloguing in Publication Data available

Library of Congress Cataloging-in-Publication Data

Nye, Nelson C. (Nelson Coral), 1907–
    Ranger's revenge : Coyote song / by Nelson C. Nye.
      p. cm.
   ISBN 0–7838–9673–5 (lg. print : sc : alk. paper)
   1. Large type books. I. Title.
PS3527.Y33 R36 2002
813'.54—dc21
                                2001039968

CHAPTER ONE

When a feller sets down to take stock on a thing it ain't no powerful hefty chore to figure out how he ought to of done. I oughtn't to of let Burt talk me into it, but I was sound asleep when he come and shook me awake in the middle of that September night.

'Rise up, Dan! We got to get busy. The governor has ordered me to swear in some Rangers—says it's the only way we can beat these crooks, an' between you an' me he's prob'ly right. I'm to have my pick of thirteen men an' I'm wantin' you should be one of them.'

I expect I done considerable blinking. In the light of his candle Burt Mossman's broad shoulders looked filled with a restless energy. His long mustaches fairly quivered and his eyes was like bright bits of gun steel. Like everyone else. I knew him for the fightin'est boss the Hashknife outfit ever had. I knew he could cuss in two languages and could play a good game of poker, but I never had dreamed he could be such a whizzer as the next twelve months was to show him. Nor did I guess what he was letting me in for.

It looked like a honor the way he put it. We hadn't never had no Rangers before. Thirteen men they was going to allow him, and he was asking me to be one of them!

Like I said, I was half asleep at the time. A feller with sense wouldn't of touched that job with the end of a forty-foot lass rope. But I never did fetch no medal for brains and I wouldn't be twenty till next year's grass and the idea of being a real gun-slogging Ranger was warming me up to a fine proud glow. It never crossed my feeble mind that the handbill boys practically run this country. I say deep down inside me I was feeling right tickled to think a man like Burt would call on me. I plumb forgot that six badge-toters in the past six months had been profanely planted in our local boot hill.

I looked up at Burt, mighty grateful. I was picturing me, Dan Waggoner, Ranger. I was thinking what a strip I was going to turn and what a hell-tearing scourge I would be to them rustlers.

I grabbed up Burt's paw and shook it.

You don't hear much about Burt no more. I expect piles of folks ain't never heard tell of him, but he was knowed in that day as a man who got results, and he sure knew how to get shed of a cow thief!

'Ninety-one is a long while back, but plenty of gents can still recall it and every blistering thing it stood for—horse-stealing, rustling, burning and lynching, cutting scrapes, gun fights, range wars and bushwhackings. Arizona was become the owl-hooter's paradise, stealing cattle was the territory's best business, and some of the ablest of the industry's practitioners had come shoving in from Texas where they wasn't no longer needed. Yet in one short year Burt changed all that. With thirteen men he tamed an empire, and all he ever got out of the deal was the pride he took in a job well done.

*   *   *

I can see mighty well on looking this over you'll be finding one thing a heap apparent. You'll of guessed by now without much trouble I ain't no kind of a book writer. I ain't even going to pretend to be. I'm just Dan Waggoner, a middlin' to honest pilgrim which has spent the bulk of his seventy-five years doing what he could from the back of a horse.

Pen wrangling, I reckon, is a heap like breaking out four-year-olds. It ain't something any guy can do overnight. I can talk about breaking horses because for a good long while it was my bread and butter. A bronc buster has to know what he's doing and a good one is hard to come by, account of you can't pick up that kind of savvy like you'd pick up a hay hand or cotton cropper. Any top hand can ride snuffy ones but, as a regular thing, you won't find them doing it. That's what the bronc buster's hired for; it is what they pay him those few extry bucks for. He's a feller that takes a

3

real pride in his work. He counts it plenty important to be knowed as his outfit's rough-string rider. You won't often find him abusing his charges. He's drawing his pay to make cow horses out of them and the feller that spoils a spread's remuda won't last no longer than a June frost does in the south of Texas.

Now here I am, you see, plumb off the trail again. No real writing feller would clutter his pages with stuff like this that don't belong in them. He would cull out all this off-branded stuff and cut it plumb back before making his tally. But it's me, Dan Waggoner, that's writing this thing and them as don't like it can quit right now.

*　　　*　　　*

Burt Mossman was watching me close like.

I said, 'Governor Murphy is showin' good sense. What is it you want I should do, Burt?'

A thin grin edged across Burt's mouth. 'I want you to pasear west a bit—up into the Tonto country. There's a heap of dark smoke blowin' down from that way an' I want to find out what's behind it. I would sure go up there myself if I could, but I got to git out on the Blue for a spell. You will have to be on your own up there, Dan. It'll prob'ly be rough. It'll be a heap colder than frogs' legs. I expect you had better take your soogans along.'

'You're anxious I should go right away are

4

you, Burt?'

'You can't git up there too quick,' Burt said. 'If the word's to be trusted, there's bad trouble brewin'. It's a big pile of country around a place called Rattlesnake Basin—there's two big outfits, Rafter an' Straddle Bug, pawin' sod over it. The basin is under the Brad and Dash iron, but the Brad and Dash boss, Hack Sloan, is missin'. He don't seem to be around no more; that's how come Murphy's havin' me send you up there. He's gettin' powerful tired of these range feuds. If there's a fuss buildin' up there he wants you to stop it.'

I looked at Burt like a kid would at his teacher. I put a nice shiny dream into words then. I said, 'A Ranger always gets his man, don't he?'

There was the start of a quirk around Burt's lips but a start was all the further it got. He give me a mighty sober nod. 'A Ranger most usually tries mighty hard.'

'An' you'll be wantin' him brought back alive, I reckon.'

'Well—if it's humanly possible, Dan,' Burt said.

There's a good bit more to being a Ranger than just going out and shooting at something. I didn't know that then. I expect I was counting that trip quite a lark. I was feeling right tall in the saddle.

I had been fetched up on cowhand talk of the hell-bending Texas Rangers. No Ranger

5

living in '91 had been bragged up one-half so free as Captain John Hughes of that outfit. All across the mountain wastes of New Mexico, West Texas, and West Otherplaces, much swollen tales of Johnny Hughes was the fashion for aftergrub yarning. Captain Johnny's record listened just like the life of old Pecos Bill; his deeds was things oft told in whispers. He was the curse of the evildoer. Every wild young sprout in the cactus that wasn't out aping Billy the Kid was plumb lathered and itching to be a John Hughes.

Johnny Hughes was a soft, low talker. He showed his teeth in a lot of fine grins; he was a man with a head on his shoulders. He never smoked nor drank nor gambled; they claim he even taught Sunday School, and he never lost a prisoner. When he joined the Rangers in '87, his corporal—a regular red-striped hell-on-wheels—got killed in a little fracas. They made John Hughes the corporal. Then some knife-wielding Mexicans slashed up his sergeant so they gave *his* job to Johnny. When, a couple years later, his captain got killed, there plainly wasn't another thing to do but to make poor John the captain.

Rangers was expected to be a heap brave. In Texas they had a saying then that a Ranger was a man with guts and a horse, and I mulled over them things as I got my stuff ready.

A Ranger, they'll tell you, never turns back. Though the odds may be a thousand to one, a

Ranger is expected to go plowing right through them, but John Hughes had showed a lot smarter than that. He had used him some Injun tactics. He had sent out scouts just the same as the crooks and he always slept with a ear to the ground. He made a study of cow thiefs and Mexicans and he come to know what they would do right smart of a while before they done it.

I was pretty ambitious in them days. I aimed to be another John Hughes.

*   *   *

On the back of a horse it takes a few days for a man to get into the Tonto country. As the crow flies maybe it ain't so far, but on a horse it's pretty much up and down going with a lot of creeks and canyons to cross, and other stout obstacles reared by nature.

The desert ranges was halfway up to your knees in grass when I set out for the Brad and Dash basin. There was poppies blooming among the six-weeks grass, Injun paintbrush and forget-me-nots. It made everything look mighty fine.

I put up that first night on Ellison Creek with an old-time don from Caborca who had ranged them hills for thirty years. He had fought off Apaches and storms and droughts but he looked for a new crowd to sheep him out. He said there was sheep crossing regular

7

now, going up to summer in the White Mountains pastures; they was due to come back, heading south, right now, feeding off what the summer rains had brought up; and this don said after them sheep got through a locust couldn't find enough to grow wings on. The old gent didn't have much to offer but he treated me like I was one of his relations.

It was October when I got to Spring Creek and could pick out the Diamond Butte mountain. It was blowing awful cold and mean and I was glad I'd thought to fetch my heavy coat. It looked like snow and felt that way and, in consequence, I was feeling right-down chipper when, just short of dark, I sighted the buildings of a ranch headquarters. It was just my luck there was nobody home; leastways nobody answered my knock or my holler. Sure, I savvied all right I'd be welcome to stay, but I reckoned I'd probably come onto another and anyways, Gisela, I figured, was somewheres close by.

But I was wrong about that or I got twisted round. It was right close onto ten when I spied what there was of Gisela. That sure wasn't much, not even for a cow town. One crosstrails store, one saloon, and two shacks that was coming bad apart at the seams, and the beetle-bored relics of a pole corral. The saloon was the only place that was lit. There was three horses hitched to its snorting post. I left mine beside them and went on in.

Three men had their bellies against a plank bar. A whiskery feller in a jumper stood back of it.

The customers turned and looked me over and turned back again and considered their whiskey.

'By grab,' I said, 'that stove sure looks good. Damn cold night to be stuck in a saddle.'

Not one of them jaspers waggled his jaw. The barkeep shifted his weight sort of nervous and his eyes said he wished he was someplace else. Then the biggest of the three, the most important looking one, a black-browed bruiser with a patch on one eye, said kinda casual, like be was talking to his drink, 'A stove don't give a damn what gits round it.'

For half a cent I would of scattered his teeth on the planking. If I'd been a free agent I'd of hit him for nothing, and I was pretty much minded to do it anyway.

I recollected Burt Mossman and smoothed down my feathers. I tromped up to the bar like I never heard the critter, but I reckon that barkeep seen how it was.

'Purty cold,' he mumbled, and set out a bottle and a glass to go with it.

I flipped him two bits and poured me out some of it. 'How far to the nearest ranch?' I said.

The guy with the eye shield said without turning, 'Nearest ranch is mine, an' I ain't hirin' drifters.'

I counted ten quick. I got a hell of a temper. I counted another ten just for good measure.

'The nearest *cow* ranch,' I said to Whiskers, and Black Patch's pals made a quick jump sideways.

The big guy pushed himself free of the bar. There wasn't no love light shining out of him. That good eye looked like a sidewinder's lantern. I took a hard grip on the neck of the bottle, kind of watching to see if he would lug out his cutter.

He didn't lug out nothing but a grating tone. 'You better cut loose of this while you're able.'

'You expectin' my health to decline?' I asked.

'Never mind,' he glowered. 'You take my advice an' git out of this country.'

'Listen, Bo Peep—'

'Aw, come on,' one of the others piped up. 'Don't waste your breath on the peckerneck, Jude. Bluff will know how t' deal with him.'

'You're right,' Black Patch nodded. 'He don't understand kindness.'

They slogged down their whiskey and tromped on out.

'Sociable gents,' I said to the barkeep. 'That their natural complexion they're sportin' or have they just got through with a hatchet raisin'?'

The barkeep shrugged and made him a sound like a balloon getting emptied. 'Bad times has sure come down on the Tonto. I

10

never seen nothin' like it before, an' man' an' boy I've lived here nigh onto forty year. Every guy an' his uncle—' He looked at me and shut up. He got a dirty rag and started rubbing his bar.

'What's it all about?' I said, real indifferent, but Whiskers wasn't swapping no small talk. 'Any chance,' I said, 'gettin' work in this country?'

He quit wiping at last and put down his rag. He put the flats of both hands on the bar edge and leaned there a while like he was tracking some varmint down in his mind. Finally he said with a shrug, 'That gent with the patch give you good advice, boy. Did I happen to be you I would sure be takin' it.'

'If there's trouble pilin' up in this country,' I said, 'I should think them hairpins would be glad of some help.'

'A feller would think so,' Whiskers agreed, and went back in a corner and set himself down.

After sulking in silence for a while I said, 'What's the nearest outfit above this locality?'

The way that feller picked up was amazing. 'You mean towards Payson?' he asked, looking friendly. 'That'll be Oxbow Hill.'

'Any chance of me gettin' put up here tonight?'

'I guess my ol' woman could fix you a shakedown.' He didn't look a heap enthusiastic about it. 'It'll cost you four bucks,' he said,

11

smiling a little.

'How far to this Oxbow Hill place?'

'Around eight or ten miles. You goin' to Payson?'

'I ain't goin' to pay no four bucks for a bed!' I got out of there then and climbed onto my gelding.

*　　*　　*

It must of been round twelve o'clock by my reckoning when the squat huddled shapes of buildings thrust themselves into my thinking as solid chunks in the black gloom around me. There had been a fair trail going north from Gisela and I'd followed it for a good half-mile before I'd swung left in an arc heading south. Such a pass wouldn't fool even halfwits long, but I reckoned it might give me a little start on trouble.

And now here I was seeing buildings again. This place was darker than a blacksmith's apron, so black I couldn't of found my face with both hands, especially under them cottonless cottonwoods. but I could tell that them blotches was buildings and I could tell by their look it was a ranch headquarters. It might, I thought, be the Bluffs' place, the Straddle Bug.

I'd been hearing a creek for a right smart while. I expect I'd been travelin' sort of right along with it; I still could hear it off beyond them buildings and that was about all I could hear. Not even the nicker of a horse to greet me nor the bark of a dog or anything. Sound sleepers, I decided, but I do remember thinking it was kind of queer for a place that big to seem so darn quiet, so squeezed out and drained of all natural noises.

A kind of unease got into me and that was when I should of skinned my eye.

I was thinking of going on over to the bunkhouse when something I smelled made me pull up my horse. It was the stinking smell of a coal-oil wick that hadn't been much more than just blowed out.

I was fixing to back my mount out of there when a sharp command come out of the quiet. 'Set right where you are! Don't move a muscle!'

I was ringed with the shapes of waiting men.

CHAPTER TWO

At another time I'd of felt like a fool being caught flat out like a tenderfoot that way. But I never felt foolish one bit right then. I felt cold fear crawl up my back.

The talker said. 'Unbuckle that belt an' let it fall.'

I done it. I done it real careful.

You could hear them let go of their breaths

plumb relieved like. The gent who'd been peddling the tongue oil said, 'Frank, git over there an' pick up his smoke pole,' and a man come edging over and done it and, quick like and careful, got out of my reach. The guy who'd been wagging his jaw said, 'All right. You can git down off that horse now, mister,' and when I did he said, 'Jones, strike a light to that lantern.'

'What the hell do we care who the stinker is?' some feller ripped out, like he could manage this better. 'All polecats look a heap the same to me. It'll sure be one of them Rafter—'

'It might be Varlance,' the first guy said, and about that time Jones got his lantern lit.

I seen mighty quick what ailed them.

There was a dead gent laying on the edge of the porch. He was all over blood and there was a knife sticking out of him.

The first guy's eyes said he knowed who done it and the way he was looking made it plain he meant me. Them other guys looked like they thought so, too, and it give me a mighty uncomfortable feeling. I had aimed to unload a good chunk of my mind, but I seen right then I would be wasting my breath. The feller was dead and I was handy and this crowd wasn't gathered to hear no arguments.

I took a look at the guy who'd done most of the talking. He was a stoop-shouldered jigger in bullhide chaps with a cast in one eye and a

14

limp to his walk. I seen him limp over and mumble some words at the guy which had figured all polecats looked similar. This gent was younger and a heap on the ringy side. He had his back humped up like a mule in a hailstorm.

'What the hell difference does that make?' he snarled. 'He's got plenty of gun sharks we ain't seen! He prob'ly hired this bird just for this piece of business. Hell's fire! Git a rope, somebody, an'—'

'Here—wait!' I said, and then I seen the girl.

She was tall and slim in a man's flannel shirt. Faded jeans snagged her hips like appleskin and pride made a fire in the look of her eyes. You couldn't guess in that light what color they was but you knew straight off there wasn't no others like them. She had her hat in her hand and corn-yellow hair run rebelliously back from a face that would start excitement anyplace.

I seen that much and then the guy said, 'Well!' like a file dragged over a rusty nail.

I give him back his look. 'It wasn't me,' I said.

'You got proof of that, hev you?'

'Sure,' I said. 'I just come from Gisela.'

'Here's a rope,' someone growled, and the young feller grabbed it. The stoop-shouldered gent mouthed a curse and reached for him. 'Keep your pants on! This feller may know

15

somethin'.'

But the young gent wasn't hunting advice. The flush on his cheeks said he didn't need none. He shook off the older man's hand with a snarl. 'Keep outa this, Tom. Get him back on that horse, Chuck. You, Vetch, help him!'

Two punchers come toward me, the two he had called to. This kid wasn't fooling. He was aching to hang me. The girl looked scared.

'This feller ain't jest been killed,' I said. 'That blood on him's dry.'

'That's a fact,' Tom said, but that dadburned kid kept a-coiling his rope.

'You don't think if I'd killed him I'd be waitin' around, do you?'

'You ain't been waitin' round. You come back after somethin',' the kid said dustily. He smeared his loop around my neck and give a good jerk on the rope to tighten it. 'Git him up on that horse, boys.'

Cold sweat come busting out all over me. I wouldn't be no good to Mossman dead.

I said, 'The governor ain't goin' to like what you're doin'.'

Them fellers quit moving like I'd dragged out a shotgun.

'Governor!' Stoop-shouldered Tom's pale eyes jumped wide open.

The young feller slammed rough talk at his punchers. 'Get him up on that horse!' The way he jerked on that rope like to of pulled loose my gullet. He sure was hellbent to get me

16

hanged.

The girl looked scared stiff.

'Wait a minute!' Tom growled.

The two punchers eased back on their boot heels and done it.

Old Tom bored me with a eye like a auger. 'What's that you was sayin' about the gov'nor?'

'You birds ever hung any Rangers before?'

The bones of Tom's face kind of swelled, it seemed like. But the kid said, 'You ain't in Texas, bucko! Texas Rangers don't mean nothin' to us!'

'Would a *Arizona* Ranger?' I asked him.

He looked like he could chew spikes and like them. You'd of thought I had told the kid there wasn't no Santa Claus. There didn't none of them look too happy about it. Old Tom looked like the wrath of God and the funny thing was he was glaring at the kid.

The kid suddenly threw back his head and laughed. 'And where would we be findin' a Arizona Ranger? What kind of sandy you tryin' to run in here?'

I said, 'Don't you guys never get around any?'

'How's that?' Tom said.

I looked at him scornful. 'Ain't none of you smart guys heard of the Hashknifes? Ain't you never heard tell of their boss, Burt Mossman?'

'How does Mossman come into it?' the kid said.

'He's their captain.' I grinned. But my fun

didn't last long. They didn't look to be no more scared about Mossman than a cat would be stopped by a fish on the table. By all the signs and signal smokes them fellers was feeling more ringier than ever.

It was plain I had got to do something quick. And it was sure going to have to be something dang forceful if I reckoned to keep myself off that rope. The crew had their wooden looks fixed on old Tom, but the old man was watching that dadblasted kid and it looked like he was going to let the kid have his way.

I could see them fellers didn't care who you was. It was what you could *do* that counted with this bunch.

I decided to show them.

'All right, kid,' I said. 'I'll give you one minute to get that rope off.'

I didn't know if I'd get by with it or not. I seen the black hate fire the kid's narrowed stare. I watched the long shape of him gather itself, bring him onto his toes and leave him there, startled. I knew what he was thinking—I knew what they was all thinking. I seen the harsh look of old Tom's Texas face and the kill-hungry shine of them watching eyes round me. Every man in that yard seen what I was up to and I looked for old Tom to stop it pronto. Shoving this play to a personal issue couldn't help nobody concerned but me. But the old man stood where he was and said nothing.

18

I looked at the kid. 'Get it off,' I told him.

A wildness rolled through that kid's saffron eyes, a look that was three shades blacker than hate.

'All right,' I said. 'You asked for it, friend.'

He come for me then with his teeth bared and snarling. I don't know what he looked for me to do but whatever it was I didn't do it. I put four knuckles right under his chin and his eyes looked like they would roll off his cheekbones. His head went back and he flung out both arms clawing wild for balance and, while he was like that, I hit him again. In the stomach this time. All the breath come out of him. He reeled and lurched forward, trying to get his arms round me. I clouted them off and hit him twice more without no mercy. He tried to get up off his back but he couldn't.

I looked at the girl. Her face was white as a sheet.

The kid rolled over and come onto his knees. He hung there a minute like he was going to pitch flat. He retched instead and come onto his feet. I seen fresh blood smeared across his mouth.

I watched the cut lip peel away from his teeth. He was licked, all right, but he wasn't forgetting. 'That's enough,' he said through the wheeze of his breathing.

'Come around here, then, and take that rope off.'

He stood where he was and shook his head.

19

'I can do it again,' I said, 'if I got to.'

A shudder run through him. He grated his teeth. By the look of his face he was still stupid with punishment. 'No,' he said, 'you won't touch me again.'

His eyes was on me but they hadn't no focus. It was like he was looking through and beyond me.

'Kid,' I said, 'I ain't begun yet. You put the rope there. Now get it off.'

He come toward me slow like. Pain had begun to get hold of his nerve ends. He put up a hand to his busted mouth and shuddered again and let the hand fall. He came up at last into the shine of the lantern, and it come over me strange like we had met before. Something about them eyes was familiar, something about the twist of his lips and the deep-etched lines that run down to his mouth.

And then I remembered.

Him and me hadn't met. I had seen that look, or one mighty like it, on a handbill over to Houston the year before. I could still see the tall black print that said WANTED and the line underneath, *For Murder and Robbery*, and then the guy's name. DALLAS JOE FINCH was the name they had on it.

This kid sure looked like Finch to me.

'Be careful,' I said.

And he was. Plenty careful. But once he'd got his damn rope off he flung it down with a curse and stamped off, disappearing at once out of reach of the lantern.

I looked at the guy that was holding my shooting iron. I give him a nod. 'I'll resume charge of that.'

He passed it over without a word.

'Now,' I said with the tone of authority, 'what place is this an' who is that dead guy?'

I put it to Tom. He looked at me blankly.

He shifted his chaw and give a hitch to his gun belt. 'All Mossman's Rangers act like you?'

'You can't fight crime with a feather duster!'

'That kid ain't crime. That's young Dandy Bluff. That's his old man over there on the porch.'

CHAPTER THREE

You could of knocked me down without half trying.

Just before I had larruped away from the Hashknife, Burt had give me a few extra details. Harry Bluff, the big boss of the Straddle Bugs, he said, was a he-kangeroo you had to handle with gloves on. He had got his raising at Flat Rock, Kentucky, and didn't care to stand for being told nothing. He was bigoted and proud; and that pride, it seemed, run all through the outfit, clean on down to the chore boy. And there, stiff and still as a five-dollar hat, lay the old gun-grabbing wolf himself in his own dried blood with a knife in his back.

And that damn kid was his son, this feller I'd thought to be Dallas Joe Finch. It was amazing. You'd of swore no two fellers could look so alike.

I was glad I hadn't shot off my mouth. It was about the only bright thing I had done so far. The guy wouldn't be loving me none as it was. By his eyes he was going to cherish that pounding.

They would all be remembering it, I guessed. I was sure getting off to a mighty large start.

I thought of some more of the things Burt had told me. This dead feller, Bluff, had been throwing his weight around, making things rough on a bunch of his neighbors. One or two of these outfits, Burt had told me, had gone and yowled to the governor about it. Some of them claimed Bluff was trying to set up an empire. It kind of struck me that maybe that was what got him killed, this craving for land that he hadn't no right to. That high-handed stuff don't set good with us Westerners.

Burt said nobody knew how much stock the Bluffs run, but they had enough land gathered under their iron to make half a dozen fair-sized spreads. They had a yarn going how Bluff was aiming to get his hands wropped around Sloan's basin. Sloan was the feller that run his cows in the Rattlesnake.

Headquartering on the Tonto, just across from the mouth of Alkali Canyon, Bluff had spread out north in a great half-circle all along the creek and past Curry Basin all along the north rim of Cocomunga Canyon. South he had gone across several more, grabbing off all the range clear to Haystack east. If he got hold of Rattlesnake he'd have the whole country, or all of the country that was any account.

That was what folks had been telling the governor.

There was just one thing between the Bluffs and that basin. And that thing was Rafter. The Rafter outfit was owned by Jim Varlance, as kind a hearted feller as you ever would see—according, that is, to what these folks had told Governor Murphy. All the two-bit crowd spoke well of the Rafter; not a man of them had a hard word for Jim Varlance. He was the salt of the earth. They couldn't find enough good things to say for him.

Governor Murphy, however, wasn't nobody's fool. He had felt, and Burt with him, like this gold heart of Varlance might be plain pyrites. All the hard words had been heaped on the Bluffs and their 'gun-throwing' riders. There wasn't nothing them fellers wouldn't lay at Bluff's door. 'Highhanded' was one of the things they called him, and a whole heap of others more fittin' to the cow camps than to a lady's withdrawing room.

Be that as it might be, Bluff was plenty dead

23

now. And it would be my chore to find out who had killed him before I could get any forwarder with the business that had fetched me up this way.

And it wasn't going to be like falling off no log. I could see that plain. These creeks was like to run plumb red and all them fires smoldering through these hills was like to blaze with a wicked fury if I didn't grab on to Bluff's killer quick. This crew standing round me would sure see to that.

I scowled down at Bluff and tried to think how Johnny Hughes would of done, but it didn't seem to help me no great amount. Being a Ranger didn't look so good now. Being on my own didn't look so good, neither.

Old stoop-shouldered Tom spit out his cud and crammed the side of his face with a fresh one. 'What are you aimin' to do about this? Standin' there glarin' ain't goin' t' help nothin'.'

I didn't like his chesty tone nor the chesty way he looked at me, neither. He was a sight too cool, too convinced and confident of his own high worth, for me to feel any leanings toward him. He was a Texas man just the same as young Bluff; he was one of them quiet and tight-lipped kind than which you'd be hard put to find tougher. He was the kind of a gent that used to ride for John Chisum.

'Suppose you unlimber your jaw a little,' I said.

He give me another of his bullypuss stares and fastened his thumbs in his gun belt. 'What are you bustin' t' hev me say?'

'Well, you might give your names. It might help some. Mine's Dan Waggoner.'

Nobody said much. The kid slouched up and stood watching me silent. The girl's frightened eyes slanched a quick look around and the crew's wooden faces stayed just like they had been.

'Fellers,' I said, 'that's scared to give out their names, has usually got some mighty good reason.'

It didn't bother Tom any, or if it did he didn't show it.

The girl pulled her eyes off the kid and said breathless, 'I'm Lovelee—Bluff's daughter,' and tried to fetch up a smile, but it kept going wabbly around the edges. You would of thought she was expecting to have a knife shoved in *her*. She looked like she wanted to say something else but she was too scared to do it.

I said, 'It's been a rare privilege to know you ma'am,' and hung a new look on that stoop-shouldered Texican.

'I'm Harry's foreman, Tom Driver,' he said grudgingly.

He didn't stick out his paw. I didn't stick out mine, neither.

'What do you know about this?' I said.

'I don't know nothin' about it.'

25

'You want to find out who put that knife in Bluff, don't you?'

'I'll find out,' he said. He looked like he meant it.

'When you do,' I told him, 'drop round an' tell me. Don't start unravelin' no cartridges. The Law will take care of that end of it.'

He didn't say if he would or he wouldn't. He didn't say nothing.

'Well, who found him?' I said when I got tired of waiting.

I seen Lovelee's shoulders give a kind of a shudder. 'We were just coming back from the—'

'Circle L,' Driver said. 'It's on Skunktracks Ridge. Luis Roblero's place.'

'Thanks,' I nodded. I turned back to the girl.

'We were just going into the house,' she said. 'Me and—' She looked at the kid. 'Me and—Dandy. I—I guess I screamed.'

'I can swear to that,' Driver told me.

I looked at the kid. 'What did you do?'

'He yelled for a lantern,' Driver said. 'Jones fetched one. We all piled over here—'

'How long was this before I showed up?'

'Mebbe ten–twelve minutes.'

I felt sorry for the girl. She wasn't in no shape to have questions chucked at her. What she was needing was to get her mind off it. She was too keyed up and she was scared besides. But it was plain I wouldn't get much from the

26

rest of them. All the help they'd give me you could stuff in your eye.

'Miz Bluff, ma'am,' I said, 'if you'll go into the house an' be fixin' a place for him—'

'Of course— Yes, I will.' Her eyes looked grateful. I had a queer notion they were trying to say something; then they just looked scared and she was hurrying off, glad to have something to do, I reckoned.

'We don't need the crew here,' I told Driver. 'You an' the kid can lug him in, can't you?'

Making sure the girl had really gone inside, I went over to the porch and got the knife out of Bluff. It wasn't a thing I had wanted her to see. She was a sight too close to hysterics already. I took the knife over to the lantern and the rest of them crowded around, watching curious. It had a stout, heavy blade and a common bone handle. If any of them knew it they wasn't letting on none.

'All right, boys,' I said, 'You can go pound your ears now.'

I watched them drift off. A light flared up inside the house. Jones took his lantern and went off with the others. I looked round through the shadows. 'Where's the kid?' I asked.

'Oh, give him a rest,' Driver said. 'That kid thought a whole lot of Harry. He'll be round again when he gits pulled together.'

I didn't reckon it made much difference which of us packed Bluff into the house. I bent down to pick up his booted feet and that was the way I stopped, bent over.

'What is it?' Driver asked.

Light spilling out through the front room window showed a dark spot at the edge of the porch. It was between Bluff's body and the ends of the planking. I struck a match and bent nearer.

Driver come up and looked over my shoulder. 'Blood!'

'Yeah.' I said, 'See can you get him turned over on his back. Not that way. Toward the wall.'

He done it. You wouldn't of looked for such care in him no way. I run my eye over the planks Bluff had laid on, observing their lines and their unspotted grayness. 'Been dead quite a spell.'

'Couple hours, mebbe.'

'What time you got now?'

'I got a quarter to one.'

I had figured Bluff dead for a good while longer but I didn't put up no argument about it. I watched Driver put the big watch in his pocket.

'About young Dandy,' I said, watching Driver. 'Been away from here much in the last couple years?'

'Away?'

'Sure—you know what I mean. Most of these young sports fiddles around some.'

'Oh!' Driver eyed me and shrugged. 'Young Bluff ain't that kind—don't give a damn for

28

the fillies. He's spent his whole life right here on the Tonto. The furtherest place he's ever been is Gisela.'

I put that notion away, plumb disgusted. If the kid hadn't never been out of this country he couldn't very well of been Finch over in Texas. I dropped the burnt match.

'Whereabouts is the quickest we can find us a saw bones?'

'Greenback,' said Driver. He was watching me odd like.

'Better get someone ridin'.'

'What for?' Driver said. He looked at Bluff again, scowling.

'You reckon he will ever git t' be any deader?'

'I'm cravin' to know what time he bucked out at.'

'What difference does that make?'

I said, 'It might make a lot to the feller that killed him.'

CHAPTER FOUR

Some sudden thought put a change in Driver's face. But he didn't say anything. He took his thumbs from his gun belt and walked off and left me.

I went into the house and took a quick look around. This was plainly the setting room,

29

though bigger and a lot better furnished than most. Setting rooms generally is cut to pattern, in the ranch country anyway, overcrowded and filled with a lot of junk their owners just hasn't the heart to pitch out. But this wasn't like that. There was cloths at the windows. It had its share of the do-funnies, too, and a couple of whatnots piled full of junk. But there was elbowroom also, and the chairs and things was made to set on, good solid oak and none of that horsehair tomfoolery to stick into you.

I got the lamp off the table and put it down on the arm of the sofa that was alongside a window that looked onto the porch. Then I went back outside and looked at the spot again.

It was blood, of course, just like Driver had said. I hadn't doubted that part. What had caught my attention was the shape and the look of it.

Bluff hadn't died right away, by the look of things. Dead guys don't bleed and Bluff had bled plenty. The knife had gone in just beneath his left shoulder. The odd thing was that most of the blood that had dried on his clothing was over the wound like he'd been laying downhill, which he wasn't.

It was a lead-pipe cinch be hadn't been stabbed on this porch. He'd been killed someplace else and packed in here dead.

There was just that one little spot. And it hadn't been under him. There wasn't no blood under Bluff at all. The spot was close to the edge where someone had tracked it when they put Bluff up here. The boot that had made it had had a cracked sole.

I looked at Bluff's boots. No cracked soles on them. Some puncher's old boot that was brushclawed and shabby. The killer, I decided, had worked in the dark and hadn't no idea he had left his boot mark.

All that figuring made me feel pretty good. I reckoned John Hughes couldn't of done no better.

But I knew mighty well there was a heap I wasn't getting. Like what was going on between Tom Driver and Dandy. Like all the look-swapping I had seen passed around, the muttered talk of the crew, the scared look of the girl. The whole damn feel of this place was wrong. There wasn't no restfulness round here at all. The whole outfit acted like they was setting on dynamite.

What had got Lovelee so dadburned scared?

Driver come back. He had the kid with him.

'Feelin' better?' I asked.

The kid looked at me black like. Driver said, 'I told Jones to get a fresh bronc an' not pick any daisies.'

'All right,' I said. 'Let's take Bluff in.'

The light coming out through the setting-room window didn't fall on nobody's face but old Harry Bluff's, but I could see well enough to know who'd do the packing. We done it, too—me and Tom Driver. That elegant kid never lifted a hand.

We took Bluff into his bedroom. The kid didn't bother to go in with us even. We were putting the old man down on the bed when horse sound boomed the planks of the bridge. Lovelee's head came round and her eyes flashed to mine.

'That's Jones goin' after the Doc,' I told her. 'When a man dies by violence you got to have a inquest.'

'He wants to find out what time Harry died.'

That was Driver, of course. I looked at him, scowling.

'But why?' Lovelee cried. 'What difference can it make?'

'It's the way Rangers work,' I said shortly. Then I seen her face and felt mean about it. I give her a smile, trying to cheer her a little. Lovelee had had about all she could take. I wanted to say something that would get that all-gone look from her cheeks, but what could you say to a girl whose father ain't much more than cold from a knife in the back?

'You go along an' try to catch some rest,' I said. 'An' then, when you're feelin' a little more perky, there's a number of questions—'

'If you got any questions—'

'When I'm wantin' your help I'll ask for it, Driver.'

He didn't like that at all. Breath swelled his

chest but he kept it inside him. He half wheeled from the room and then come back, scowling.

I said to Lovelee, 'How long's he been with you?' I give a jerk of my thumb at Driver.

'Tom?' Her eyes was like burnt holes in a blanket. 'Tom's all right.'

She shivered again and her eyes raked across my face kind of wild like. 'I wished you'd tell me what you're scared of,' I said, and it almost seemed like her face got paler.

'I'm not scared,' she said. 'It's just— Wouldn't *you* be upset if your Dad had died that way?'

There wasn't no answer to that. I nodded. 'Suppose you tell me what's been going on around here.'

She stared at me blankly.

'Tell him about Jim Varlance,' Driver said.

She clenched her hands and wouldn't meet my look. 'We've been having some trouble with Jim Varlance's outfit,' she said. 'Not really trouble, but—there's been talk. You know how things are in a country like this. Jim runs the Rafter; next to us it's the biggest. He headquarters off to the east of Bear Head Mountain. He's been getting ambitious. He's got some of the smaller spreads to throw in with him—' She broke off, looked at Driver. 'They've formed some kind of a pool, or something. Everything east of the Brad and Dash—that's Hack Sloan's iron in Rattlesnake

Basin. Hack's gone off someplace. No one—
no one knows where he is.'

She looked up and then down, too quick for
me to get it, but I'd of swore her eyes was
trying to tell me something, 'Of course,' she
added worriedly, 'you needn't take my word.'

'He understands that,' Driver said.

I ignored him, 'Do you think Jim Varlance
might of killed your Dad?'

'No— Oh, no, of course not!' Lovelee cried,
going white. 'Jim's not—'

She let the rest trail away with her cheeks
suddenly hot and stared down at the floor; and
I guessed something then. I guessed she had
once thought a lot of Jim Varlance.

'Is this his knife?' I said, holding it out to
her.

'No—oh, no!' She shrank away from it. 'Jim
doesn't have a knife—I mean he never carries
one.'

I seen Driver's lip curl. 'Tell him about
yesterday.'

Lovelee looked at me miserably and twisted
her hands. 'Dad—Dad told Jim yesterday to
stay off Hack's range—warned him off. It was
hateful. Jim accused Dad of wanting Hack's
range for himself. He said if the truth was
known the Bluffs could tell why Hack wasn't
around no more. I looked for Dad to shoot
him right then. He was so mad he could hardly
talk. He said he would kill the first Rafter
hand he caught east of Tailpiece—that's Del

34

Widney's saloon at Tin Can Springs.'

'What did Jim say to that?'

'He allowed he could handle a rifle himself,' Driver growled, quick and harsh, before Lovelee could answer.

'That right?' I asked, and she nodded, miserable.

'A fine large business,' I said, disgusted. I was sure going to have my work cut out. There ain't nothing in the West that will sooner start trouble than for some guy to fling up a deadline. It beats all the fighting words ever invented. I could see mighty well how Jim Varlance would feel. Bluff, raising that deadline, hadn't left him no choice. He would have to go into Sloan's basin now; the things folks was thinking would make him go into it. A deadline's a challenge.

I would of bet anything you wanted to name there was Rafter cattle in the Rattlesnake now.

I was reminded of Dandy, how he'd wanted to hang me, how he'd been so damned sure I was on Rafter's payroll.

No wonder they all thought Varlance had killed Bluff! It would be the natural thing for some guys to do, the desperate act of a man forced to fight.

But was Varlance the kind that would kill with a knife?

I couldn't know that. But I could see well enough now why Lovelee was scared. Whether she thought he had killed her father or not she

35

couldn't help seeing that others would think so.

'Your brother,' I said, 'is a heap impulsive.'

She looked at me funny. She pulled her eyes away quickly. She looked down at the floorboards and didn't say nothing.

You could hear a clock ticking. It might of been Driver's watch in his pocket. Lovelee pulled up her chin and said in a sort of breathless way, 'He's changed. What I mean is—' She threw out her hands. She looked scared and desperate.

'We're all changed,' Driver said. 'Harry's death's been a shock to us.'

'Well,' I said, trying to get her mind off it, 'what about this Brad and Dash feller—this Sloan that seems to of turned up missing? Is he friendly with you folks? Was he friendly with Varlance? What do you know about—'

'Nothing,' Lovelee said, and grimly stared at the floor. 'I don't know anything. I—I can't talk any more.'

'You want to see that damn knifer caught, don't you?'

'I don't know what I want.' She wouldn't look at me. 'We don't even know you're a Ranger—we don't know anything about you at all.'

'You can take my word for it.'

'Well, if you are you're here to find out about Sloan—'

'And whatever you do,' Driver tucked in

36

smoothly, 'you are bound to help one side and hurt the other. How do we know which side will get hurt?'

'I'm tryin' to help *you*,' I told Lovelee.

'But a Ranger can't take sides.' That was Driver again.

'A Ranger can dig out the truth,' I said.

'But how do we know who the truth will help? Mebbe the truth would be better forgotten.'

'Driver,' I said, 'will you keep your mouth outa this?'

Lovelee put out a hand. She came toward me and touched me. 'You *do* want to help.'

'Of course,' I said simply.

All of a sudden we might of been there alone. Only her nearness seemed to matter. I put out a hand. She backed off from me, trembling. Her face had gone white again, strange and frightened.

She brought up a smile. It was small and uncertain. But it showed she had guts. She came nearer, a little. I could smell the lavender perfume she used. 'Would you do something for me—something big and—and fine?'

Driver's spurs, just then, made a grind on the floorboards. A chair seat creaked in the other room.

Her eyes stayed on me. 'Would you?' she said. She reached out, caught my fingers. She was suddenly urgent.

37

I wanted to say I'd do anything for her, anything within reason. But my mouth was dry. I was wary again. I was Burt Mossman's Ranger. What was this she was up to?

'What is it you want me to do?' I asked.

Her hand fell away.

'Go on, tell him, girl,' Driver said. 'See what he'll say to it.'

But the moment was gone. She looked wretched and miserable. She walked out of the room without speaking.

Driver followed her, and I was left alone with the lingering smell of her perfume.

CHAPTER FIVE

Swearing under my breath I went after them.

The kid was sprawled in a hide-bottomed chair. Driver stood by the mantel with his squinched-up eyes like a couple of agates. Lovelee stood by the window staring out at the dark.

I fetched out the makings and rolled up a smoke. I wished there was something I could get my teeth in. This was a heap too much like shoving through spiderwebs. Driver's dark face was blank as a bullet. The kid looked sullen. He hadn't forgot that beating I'd give him.

It was starting to rain.

'Well,' I said, 'we better get down to cases. I

been sent here to do a job of work and I reckon to do it, with your help or without it You can lie if you want. You can probably fool me. But sooner or later I'll get to the truth, an' the closer you stick to that truth as you know it the quicker I'll get my work done an' be out of here.'

I got out a match and fired up my cigarette. I rested my shoulders against a wall and that way, smoking, I stood a while watching them, wondering what hates and what hopes might be twisting them. I listened to the dismal rain on the roof boards and wondered what kind of people these were. I wondered about a good many things, standing there. I thought of the mess this Jim Varlance was in.

'Well,' I said gruffly. 'One thing you folks want to remember. There's no one so smart he can beat the Law.'

Driver curled his thin lips in a grin.

I nodded. 'A Ranger can die just like anyone else.'

That was what he was thinking. It was there in his eyes.

There was a nastier look in the kid's sullen stare. It wasn't a look I'd of took off everyone. But the guy *was* tore up, you could tell that. Moreover, he was Lovelee's own brother.

'Yes, a Ranger can die just like anyone else,' I told Driver again, 'but the Law don't forget. For every Ranger that's dropped there'll be another sent out.'

The kids thin face sneered. He chucked a glance at Tom Driver. 'You reckon he come up here to tell us that?'

'I come up here,' I said, 'to find Hack Sloan.'

'You won't find him around here!' Lovelee's brother said.

'Comin' into this country,' I said to Driver, 'I put up one night with a Mexican rancher. He didn't have a whole lot but he made me feel welcome. I'm wonderin' why I ain't welcome here.'

That touched young Bluff. He come out of his chair like the wrath of God. 'If you don't like it here fork your horse an' git out!'

Driver said from the mantel, 'Take it easy—take it easy. Hard words never buttered no parsnips. A Ranger puts up where he finds it handy. When a feller's been murdered a Ranger don't care whose hand held the pistol—'

'Or the knife,' I said. 'When a man lets his temper fly loose an' run haywire—'

The kid flung around like he would bust in my face. 'Are you tryin' to make out I killed my own father?'

'No,' I said, 'I'm tryin' to get it across to you why I'm here, an' why I'm like to be round here a good while yet. When a man lets his temper run haywire—like you do—lets his wrongs rile him up an' push him into a killin', the Rangers has got to ride, no matter. Your

40

dad, Mister Bluff, was murdered, an' murder is one of a Ranger's first interests. I come here to find Sloan, like I already told you, but now that will have to wait till I find who shoved that knife in your father.'

'If that's all you're waitin' on,' the kid said, sneering, 'a trip to the Rafter—'

'Dandy!' Lovelee whipped around, her face white. 'You've—'

'Well, it's true enough, ain't it? Nobody else had any reason to kill him.'

And Driver, though not looking to like it much, nodded. 'That's about the size of it, Waggoner.'

'When did you first discover Sloan was gone?' I asked.

Driver rubbed at his jaw and made out to look thoughtful. 'Nobody seems to know much about it. He appears to have been missed about five weeks ago.'

'It was right after Dandy went up to Gisela,' Lovelee said like she knew all about it. 'I went over to take Hack a pie I had baked. There was nobody home. I went back a week later and the pie was still there.'

Dandy looked at her like he plain didn't believe it. 'Funny you never said nothin' about it.' He scowled and his voice dropped. 'You couldn't leave no pie around here that long.'

'You forget,' she told him, 'Hack hadn't any help.'

'I was thinkin' of the rats.'

41

'But he hadn't any rats. Don't you remember how he got them all cleared out of there?'

Dandy's look was tight. 'You do take up with the damndest people.'

'He was a nice old man!'

'He was a plain damn fool!'

'After all,' Driver said like a man fed up with it, 'where's the good wranglin' over a feller we don't even know where he is at? Hack was all right. A pretty good duffer according to his lights.'

The kid flung himself in his chair again, scowling. The lamp-glow struck a brassy shine off his cartridges. There was something weird in the way Lovelee stood half turned and regarded him. She looked almost ugly, like a witch or something with her shoulders crouched that way and the lamplight piling up the shadows in her face.

'Lets get back to that party,' I said, eyeing Driver. 'You'd all been over to this Circle L outfit—what did you say that feller's name was?'

'Roblero,' Driver said. 'Don Luis Roblero—he's a Californian—'

'What was he doin'? Havin' a hoedown or somethin'?'

'He was throwin a jamboree for his daughter. She got married today.'

'How far away is his place from here?'

Driver said kind of careful, 'About thirteen

mile.' He watched me a moment, then he said like a schoolmarm, 'It's west of Pine Mountain. About a mile south of Chalk. In a straight line runnin' east by south it's about eight miles from right here where we're settin'. But you can't go like that. You got to waggle around some.'

'Who was there—just you folks?'

'The whole country was there.' growled the kid, impatient. 'Every guy an' his uncle.'

'Any of you have any trouble with Varlance?'

They looked at me sharply. There was plenty of thinking. You could feel it like drafts curling up round your shinbones. You could see it in the hammer-beaten look of their faces.

'Well, did you or didn't you?'

The kid's lips curled. He made a sound like a laugh but there wasn't no fun in it. Driver said, 'No.'

'Did you swap any talk?'

'Jim Varlance wasn't there,' Lovelee said with her face blank.

'You mean he wasn't asked?'

'There wasn't nobody asked that wasn't known friends of ours.'

I thought of her father laying dead in yonder. 'Why didn't your Dad go?'

The queer look crossed her cheeks again and her fingers plucked at the fringed buckskin gauntlets she had folded over the front of her belt. Outside the rain slogged down with new fury, beating the yard's packed ground like hoofbeats, running off the roof in a steady torrent.

'But he did,' Lovelee said like she was just now hearing me. 'I mean he—' She was looking at Dandy and she quit right there like her breath had run out.

It wasn't no look of the kid's that had stopped her; the kid wasn't paying her no mind at all. It was something in her head that had broke her talk off. When she made up her mind about it, she would go on, I thought; and she did.

'He started off with us. But after a while he remembered something he had meant to do or forgotten to bring. He said he would have to go back for a little. He said he'd be joining us later at the party.'

'Was he in good spirits?'

That kind of surprised them. You could see them considering it, turning it this way and that in their minds. 'He looked tired,' Lovelee said with her eyes still thinking.

'Anyone else notice anything?'

None of them answered.

'What time did he get to Roblero's?' I asked.

Lovelee shook her head. 'He never did.'

'Never? Never got there at *all*?'

She looked at me drearily. 'No,' she said through the sound of the rain beating down on the roof boards.

You could tell by the shine at the edge of her lashes how close she was come to outright tears. I felt for her strongly, I wanted to spare her. But Time was a man with a sharp pair of spurs. I kept seeing the news of Bluff's death speeding round. I could see the grim faces bent over their pistols; I could see rough hands gripping Winchester rifles. Time was a-crowding. I had to get at the truth. It was buried here somewhere—some part of it was. These people was trying to hide it away from me. I could tell by their answers, by the poker-faced way they kept watching me.

*   *   *

I went to the door and pitched out my smoke. The cold damp drone of the rain washed in. I shoved the door shut and it went back to its drumming.

'I'll try to speed this up but I've got to ask questions. Nobody's rushin' to volunteer nothin'.'

'There's nothin' to volunteer,' Driver said. We come back like we told you an' found Harry dead.'

'All right,' I said. 'What's the rest of it? Don't tell me there ain't nothin' more. I know better. You're a heap too anxious to be sayin' good-bye to me. I wasn't born yesterday.'

Driver shrugged. Nobody else did anything.

'All right,' I said, turning back to the girl.

'What time did your father decide to come home? What time did he leave you?'

You could see how she tried to pull herself together. It was like a knife in your heart to watch her that way. I gritted my teeth. 'What time?' I said.

She looked confused, frightened, nervous. She thought it was around seven o'clock, she said.

'Before or after?'

I had to keep plugging or I wouldn't get anywhere. I didn't know myself what I was trying to dig up here. I was like a fool kid in a creek turning stones.

'Before or after?'

'I don't know,' she said.

'An' whereabouts was this? What part of the range?'

'It was after we'd crossed Gun Creek.'

'How long after?'

'We'd just crossed it. I—'

'That creek don't go through the Brad and Dash, does it?'

'A part of it does.'

'Did you reach that part?'

Her nod was reluctant. I could see why it might be. They had been in Rattlesnake Basin when Bluff got his sudden urge to come home.

'You didn't think he might mebbe be figurin' to visit Hack Sloan's, did you?' I went on.

Lovelee's eyes come wide open. Dandy

46

cried, 'I believe you got it!' and Driver's cold jaw clamped shut like a wolf trap.

I looked at him grim like. 'You claim Bluff warned Varlance to stay out of that basin. How many folks know that?'

'He didn't make no secret of it. He told Varlance that right in town. There was plenty guys heard it.'

'I'm surprised you didn't wonder if that wasn't where he was goin' when he passed out that line about havin' to go home.'

Lovelee looked at me, baffled. 'Why all this talk of the Brad and Dash? Dad was killed right here.'

I said, 'Was he?' and saw the red line of her lips leave her teeth. Her eyes flew to Driver.

The kid said, 'Wasn't he?'

'That's one of the things I aim to find out. Right now we don't know where he was killed.'

'He couldn't of got very far with that knife—'

'He could of been *lugged* quite a ways,' I said, watching them. 'What time did the rest of you get there?'

I could tell right off I had hit on something. I could tell by the tightening lines in their faces.

'Well,' I said, '*about* what time?' I looked at Lovelee.

'We—we didn't all get there together.'

'Well, ma'am, what time did you get there?'

'Around eleven, I think.'

I looked at her sharp like.

'It took you four hours to ride seven miles?'

Her cheeks kind of trembled. Her eyes slid away from me. 'I stopped by to look in on Jude's mother. She's been down again with the shakin' fever.'

'Who is Jude?' I asked.

'Jude Strump!' Dandy spit out the words like they was worms he'd bit into.

'Strump owns the Boxed K,' Driver said. 'It's a cow spread.'

'Where is it?'

'It's up by the Gallups near the Pleasant Valley trail.'

I looked again at Lovelee. I thought she was lying. 'How long was this after your Dad left the bunch—I mean, how long after he left before you left?'

'I don't—' Color rushed into her cheeks. 'Ten minutes, I think. It might have been less—I don't know—I don't remember.'

'Did it come to your mind he might run into Jim Varlance?'

'Hell's fire!' Dandy snarled. He jumped up looking wrathful. 'Quit houndin' her, damn you! If you got t' ask questions you kin ask 'em of me.'

'All right,' I said. 'Did *you* think he might?'

'I didn't think nothin' about it.'

'What time did you get to that party?'

I seen Lovelee's eyes throw a quick look at Dandy. The kid looked like he hadn't no

48

intention of answering. Driver backed his look up. 'We don't hev to set here an' answer your questions.'

'That's right,' I said. 'Do you want me to draw my own conclusions?'

Driver's look wasn't friendly.

The kid took his sullen face round the room. He come back in a moment and looked at me tough like. 'What was that you was askin'?'

'I said what time did you get to that party.'

'I dunno—pretty late. I reckon it was just a few minutes before Lovelee.'

I put both hands on my hips and stared.

'Did you have a nice time?'

'I was huntin' a horse,' Dandy told me, scowling.

'What time did you leave the rest of the crowd?'

'I dunno, an' I don't give a damn!'

'He left just before Dad did,' Lovelee said.

I looked at the kid. I looked at Lovelee and Driver. I looked back at the kid, trying to think where this was going. I seen a damn good chance Bluff and him had got together and gone off by themselves to get rid of Jim Varlance.

I looked out of the window. It would soon be daylight.

I looked at Tom Driver's Texas face and Dandy's Texas face beside it. I thought of the face of Joe Finch on that handbill. 'Which one of you quit your outfit first?'

The kid's lip curled. He said, 'I did,' and his look invited me to make something of it.

'When did your horse get away?' I said, trying to hold down my temper.

'He didn't get away. It was a horse a guy had I was thinkin' of buyin'. The directions he give me was all boggled up an' when I finally got over there it was just a damn broomtail. He told me about a good dun east of Bear Head. I went over there. It wasn't no account either.'

I looked at Tom Driver. 'What happened to you?'

'What do you mean what happened to me?'

'Where'd you gallop off to?'

'I didn't gallop no place.'

'You went straight to Roblero's?'

Driver looked me over quite a while before answering. 'I went over there, all right, but not until later. I had work t' ketch up on—paper work. I didn't git through here till around nine o'clock.'

'That blowout must of been a big success! How long did you stay?'

'I left when the rest did.'

'That ain't what I asked you.'

Lovelee said, 'I was worried about Dad— about him not showing up. No one had seen him since he started for home. I was scared something had happened.'

'I told her,' Driver said, 'he'd prob'ly run into somethin'.'

50

'Did you tell her,' I said, 'he had run into a knife?'

Driver looked mad enough to crawl my hump. Then he smoothed his face out. He started to say something and changed his mind.

I said to the kid, 'You left with the rest. What time was it?'

'Do you think I go round with a clock in my fist?'

'Mebbe it would be a good thing if you did!'

The kid glared. I glared back. Over by the mantel Tom Driver glared, too, which made it pretty near unanimous.

Lovelee started to turn and, still turning, went rigid. Her eyes jumped at me, dark and round. I heard it, too—we all heard it then, the larruping pound of a bronc's fast travel. It crossed the bridge like a rattle of thunder. It wasn't the Doc; it couldn't be Jones, either. It clouted the gravelly shale and come on. A shout tore across the rainswept dark.

Driver jumped for the door.

We was right on his heels when he got it open. The Straddle Bug crew was a bunch of black shapes. I seen one of them yank the guy out of his saddle. An arm flashed up with a shine of metal. I yelled: 'Bring that man up here!'

Through the rush of the rain you could hear them growl. In the light spilling out of the open doorway you could see the glint of their

51

teeth, of their eyeballs. They come shoving him forward, cursing and growling like a pack of dogs.

Lovelee come out with the lamp off the table. It picked out the sodden shape of the rider. Driver caught the guy's shirt at the chest and twisted. 'You're a little bit offa your range ain't you, Cancho?'

You could see the guy's eyes rake across our faces. They landed on me and come into sharp focus. 'I guess you're the feller,' he said across Driver. 'Drumm wants you over there right away.'

'Over where?' I said.

'You're the Ranger, ain'tcha?'

'So what if he is?' Driver growled; and I nodded.

'You're the feller Drumm sent me after then —Drumm's bossin' the Rafter. He wants you to git over t' Sloan's ranch pronto. Jim Varlance is dead—somebody opened the back of his skull with a pistol.'

CHAPTER SIX

Lovelee's eyes was almost black and Driver looked like he was hacked from wood by a guy that didn't care how he done it, but the kid's high-boned and handsome face showed a brightening look of surprised satisfaction.

52

'Varlance dead!' he said. 'That's somethin'!'

You could of pushed me over with your littlest finger.

I'd expected this, but not this quick. I'd expected it because I knowed that feuds, like everything else, run generally speaking, pretty much to a pattern. I'd been sure when Harry Bluff's Straddle Bugs got their steam up there'd be hell to pay and no pitch hot. Killing breeds killing just like ticks breed ticks, but what I couldn't get through my head was how this bunch had got going so fast. Why, they hadn't but hardly got home from Roblero's. It didn't look like they could of known about Bluff until they'd got home and found him here. How the hell they could ever of got back to Sloan's basin—

'Count your crew,' I told Driver. 'See if anyone's missing.'

He counted noses and grunted. 'They're all here but Jones.'

I could see, all right, how Jones might of sidetracked on his way to fetch the sawbones. I could see mighty well how he might of killed Varlance. But I was damned if I could see how he'd known where to find him. I was commencing to wish I had never met Mossman.

'What's your handle?' I said to the Rafter hand.

He cuffed back his hat and grinned up at me tough like. 'Cancho Moran.'

The kid come up, scowling.

The rain beat down like hail and quit.

'Where'd you find Jim Varlance?'

'Rattlesnake Basin.'

The kid rose up like the tail of a scorpion. I shoved him back with no politeness. 'Take it easy,' I said. 'Whereabouts in the basin?'

'Sloan's ranch like.'

'Why, you gun-slick hound,' snarled the kid, swelling up, 'didn't my ol' man tell—'

'I'm goin' to tell *you* in a minute,' I said. As it was I was minded to hit him. Every time I looked at that glowering face I thought of the face of Joe Finch on that handbill. It didn't improve my temper none, neither. 'Now keep outa this an' keep your trap shut.'

I watched Moran search his clothes for the makings. I tossed him mine, knowing his was wet. I give him some matches. He was cool all right; he was cool as a well chain.

I said, 'How did you know there was a Ranger up here?'

'Didn't,' Moran muttered, cupping a match. 'It was Drumm. Drumm said, "There's a Ranger at Bluff's—git over there an' fetch him".'

Maybe it was his ways that made the guy seem such a cold potato. It give me the chills the chance he was taking, coming to this outfit to report the killing of a man Bluff had hated in a place Bluff had told that man never to be. I wondered if this guy knew Bluff was dead. It didn't seem too likely; still, if Varlance had killed him—

I wondered about a whole lot of things as I watched him swing himself back in the saddle. Then I shrugged it off. I looked at Tom Driver.

'There's somethin' about this business that stinks,' I said.

'Why'n't you brush it off with your feather duster?'

'There's a pile of things due to get brushed off,' I replied. 'An' the first buck I catch with a gun in his fist is goin' to Be wishin' he never was borned! Is that plain?' I said, glaring round at their faces.

It was plain enough they got the idea. It was pretty plain, too, that they wasn't liking it.

I waved them away and took a look at the kid. He hadn't got more than a sprinkle on him, having stayed on the porch till the rain had about quit. It wasn't no wonder folks called him 'Dandy'. He was got up like he worked for a carnival. He wore a ten-gallon hat that was patterned on cream. His shield-fronted shirt was red as fire and, where most folks favored a dark kind of pants, the kid's was sort of plaid effect with the brown and white squares big enough to play checkers on. He wore Texas spurs with Mexican danglers that played him a tune every time he turned round. He wore an extry broad belt, fancy stitched like his boots which had cost cash money and had come from Coffeyville. He wore his scarf pulled tight in a knot at his throat instead of like most guys with the knot around back.

He was a sure enough dude and spoiled plumb rotten, to judge from his actions.

'Tomorrow night,' I told Driver, 'we're goin' to be holdin' a meetin' here of all the owners that was at that shindig—includin' Roblero. Get the word passed round. An' you can say for me I'll be almighty suspicious of any gent discoverin' a more important schedule.'

Without waiting for no answer I went over and fetched the rope off my saddle. I ducked inside the corral bars then and, though it was still kind of dark to see real good, it not being yet quite four o'clock, I managed to snag a ewe-necked dun that looked to be built for considerable endurance. It was like pulling in a bigmouth bass. He sure done his best to tangle my twine as he hiked with the rest for the pen's far corner. But I showed him I meant business and he come along pretty fair after that. I took down the bars and led him out and, afterwards, put them up again. Then I got my rig and cinched up quick and slipped my spade bit into his mouth while he was rolling his eyes and blowing at me. I've always been a loose-rein rider, but I also like to move when I want to and a spade bit will move the meanest bronc. I got on this one and rode to the porch and left him there on grounded reins.

'Back in a minute,' I said to Moran.

I expect he'd of liked a fresh mount himself but, riding into strange country with him, it looked to me like a whole heap smarter to let him fork the one he'd come on. When I ride with someone I like to *ride* with him. Maybe I was born with a suspicious nature, but I had only his word that Jim Varlance was dead. It was quite in the cards that Varlance wasn't. I just didn't aim to take extry chances.

Lovelee had gone inside again. I found her standing by the setting-room window. She looked dog-tired and I guess she was but her face changed when she seen me, softening kind of, all of the dullness doing out of it; then it changed again, cracking up into lines of fear.

'Dan!' she cried. 'You've got to—'

Metallic sound sliced through her talk, the big-roweled clank of Dandy's spurs; and she whirled and quit the room as he entered.

The kid's eyes looked like a couple of marbles. 'I thought you was larrupin' off t' see Varlance.'

'I am,' I said, ignoring his look. 'Do you want to go with me?'

It was the first time I'd noticed the color of his eyes. Amber they was, like the eyes of a cat. Still and unwinking.

I tossed him the knife. 'Ever see that before?'

He give it a look and tossed it back. 'I dunno,' he said. 'That's the one you pulled outa the ol' man, ain't it?'

I went over and rested my hip on the table. I rolled up a smoke while I set and considered him, alert to the distrustful hostility that surrounded the man like a smell surrounds horses. He had a thinness of body that matched the thin shortness of his unstable temper. He had a wicked excitability that was all the time heating just under the surface, building up to explode at the least provocation. His good-looking face was sullen and twisted with the unsatisfactory things he was thinking. There was not much to like in the look of that kid. He wasn't the kind I'd of chose for a brother to a girl as sweet and wholesome as Lovelee.

I crushed out my smoke and stood free of the table. I picked up the knife and thrust it into my belt. 'When the doc gets here send him after me.'

Hate was in the look that damn kid flung me.

I made out not to notice. Outside I talked to Moran a moment. Light from the house made a shine in the puddles. It was damp and cold and a wind was rising.

I was fixing to climb up into my saddle when the kid come out and put a hand on my arm. He was breathing hard. The tone of his voice was black and grating.

'Keep your hands off Lovelee! Keep away from her—hear me? She ain't for the likes of no snoopin' Ranger!'

I clamped my jaws and climbed into the saddle. I picked up the reins with a nod a Moran.

'Keep on like you're goin',' the kid snarled after me, 'an' they'll put you to bed with a pick an' shovel!'

CHAPTER SEVEN

In the first gray light of a colder morning, we passed the dark slope of Felton Mountain. Our way led now up and down through foothills that were covered with shale and a variety of cactus—cholla, and barrel, and green clumps of prickly pear with now and again the wandlike stems of wolf's candle, their thorns still hid in the yellowing leaves. There was very little grass, although we saw some scrawny underfed cattle that scuttled away like they never would of done had there been any cover they could of hidden away in. Wild critters like that are a heap like deer and will take to the brush at the first sign of danger.

'Whose stuff is that?' I asked, and Moran said indifferently, 'Some of the pool stuff that got missed in the gather.'

Half an hour later we crested a rise and I got my first look at Rattlesnake Basin. It was a vast mountain meadow that was lush with grass.

Antelope fled from our path like shadows. There was piñon ahead and juniper and cedar. Ten feet to our left a covey of quail roared out of the brush and a chaparral cock sprinted off ahead of us. The sun come rocking over the bluffs and threw its red light across the pine-clad uplands and cowbirds commenced their morning chatter. It was hard to think of murder then.

I scowled at Moran and wished I was like him. He was riding along as unconcerned with danger as though he owned every step of the way. He was contentedly whistling snatches of *Red Wing* and swinging his quirt like it was nothing to him whether school kept or not. And I don't reckon it was. He didn't have no more worries than any other damn drifter and if things got too tough he could always move on. No property anchored his kind down, no scruples of loyalty tied them, neither. They was birds of passage, free as the air.

'Moran, how old are you?' I asked.

He curled back his lips in a silent chuckle. 'That won't tell you how Bluff got that knife in him.'

'No,' I said, 'I guess not,' and quit talking.

And this was the job I had felt so good about. How had this drifter known Bluff had been knifed? Had he known it before he had come to the Straddle Bug?

Probably not, I thought. He had probably

learned it from some of Bluff's crew. I remembered the way Driver's men had jumped him.

'How long have you been in this country?' I said.

He looked it all over, kind of shrugged and said nothing.

'How long you been workin' for Rafter, then?'

'About long enough t' know better, I reckon.'

'Your crowd ever had any trouble with Sloan?'

Moran grinned at me sourly. 'That Brad and Dash feller? Hell, no. We're backin' his play. My boss an' him is thicker than fiddlers— that's how come we moved our stuff into the basin. If we hadn't I reckon that Straddle Bug bunch would of carted the place plumb away by this time. You got to watch them fellers like you would a hawk.'

The comparison seemed to tickle him some way. 'What do you make of young Dandy?' I asked.

'Don't you know him,' Moran said, shaping a smoke from makings he coolly took out of my pocket.

'Who do you reckon killed Bluff?'

'Don't know that, neither.'

'Who do you think killed Varlance?'

'Hell,' Moran said, 'lemme ask you one. Who killed Cock Robin?'

I wasn't in no mood to entertain humor. I scowled at him. 'How did Drumm find out there was a Ranger at Bluff's?'

'If you're cravin' t' know you better ask him.'

I give up trying to get anything out of him. We come to a creek and splashed through it.

'Gun Crick,' Moran said, and whistled *Red Wing* again.

I said, 'That the only piece you know?'

He run off a few variations, cupping his hands like he was playing a mouth harp and putting a heap of fanciness in it.

He give up *Red Wing* after a while and we rode through the bird-twittering quiet, through the sunlight and shadows of the cool crisp morning, with only the creak of our saddle gear and the soft fall of horse hoofs to tell we was any place round there.

It was starting out well for a pleasant morning, and the sky with them evergreens rearing against it was a picture to please any eye but a drifter's. It would of been a rare treat was I riding with Lovelee instead of Moran and my thoughts for company.

My thoughts was a heap like a horse on a treadmill. They kept going around but they didn't get any place. They was sort of loping round Bluff at the moment. I was thinking he might actually have gone home last night. I had nothing but Driver's own word that he hadn't. It was quite in the cards that Tom

Driver was lying.

Still, it didn't seem likely. A rancher don't hire a guy for his foreman without he figures he can trust the feller. Just the same I didn't like it. Driver had stayed home—or at least he said he had. He said he had stayed at the ranch till round nine. You'd of thought he would have left that work for another night. Places is few to go in such country and when some spread throws a party that way mostly everybody figures to be there.

I wondered if Driver had stayed home by arrangement. If the reasons for his staying wasn't orders from Bluff. Supposing Driver and Bluff had gone off to hunt Varlance . . .

It could be, by grab!

But then what about the kid and his cockeyed story of hunting a horse? And Lovelee with her tale of visiting the Strump woman?

I scowled mighty bitter at the horn of my saddle. This was the job I had been so proud of. Then I thought of the boot track in blood on the porch. Old boots, like enough, with run-down heels. Puncher's boots, likely worn too steady to be left off for fixing.

I looked at Moran's. They was brush-clawed but sturdy. There wouldn't be any cracked soles on them. But I reckoned next time he stepped down I would have a look anyway.

Maybe the Straddle Bug boys was right; maybe one of Jim Varlance's Rafter crowd had killed Bluff. It was the obvious thing for a man to figure. I expect that's why I didn't much care for it. The Rafters would of knowed they'd be the the first ones suspected. Maybe they just didn't give a damn. They was bound to of seen they had a fight coming up and maybe, that way, they'd figured to get in first lick. First lick and last with a single shot.

Only Bluff hadn't been shot. Bluff had been knifed.

The whole damn works was a first-class headache.

And who had killed Varlance?

Where, too, was Hack Sloan?

I thought of the way that kid had come after me, telling me tough to keep away from his sister. That was coming it pretty rough. I had figured to see a heap more of Lovelee, and I still aimed to do it. But one thing, anyway, was shaping up plain. The kid hadn't forgot that beating I'd given him and he would sure make me ache if he could find a chance to.

*   *   *

'Your name Waggoner?'

'Yeah. You're Drumm?'

We had just rode up to Sloan's buildings and this guy had come out of the house with a rifle. He was a chunky burly-built block of a man with arms that would of looked about right on a blacksmith and legs I would like to of had for fence posts. What I mean he was *built*, and no fat on him any place. I expect I stared a heap harder than called for.

'So you're the Ranger.'

We looked each other all over again. His clothes wasn't much but his face had the look of a man who gives orders. It was a cold-jawed look like you sometimes get from a last year's bronc.

'Most of the time I'm the Rafter wagon boss.' He looked at the hang of my gun, at my fingers. At the rig of my horse and my seat in the saddle.

'It's the man that's the Ranger,' I said, 'not the outfit.'

'We figured they'd send a older hand.'

'I been weaned.' I said. 'How'd you know where to find me? How'd you know I'd be up there?'

He fished a cigar butt out of his pocket and stuck it between the hard grip of his teeth. 'We had a note from the gov'nor—'

'The governor didn't know what my name is!'

'Didn't he?' Drumm's smoky eyes showed no more expression than you'd find on a toenail. 'You want to see Jim now?'

It was plain that hard looks was wasted on him.

'When was this killin' discovered? Who found him?'

'I found him,' Drumm said. 'Around ten

o'clock.'

'Where?'

'Right here—we ain't moved him. If you'll step—'

'If he's dead,' I said, 'he'll keep a while longer. How many cattle have you got in this basin?'

Drumm thought that over. He stood silent, considering. 'I expect pretty close to three thousand head.'

'That's quite a passle of cattle.' Only yesterday Bluff had told these guys to stay out of here. 'You didn't lose any time.'

'Didn't figure to,' Drumm said. 'You wanta look at Jim now?'

'When I do,' I said, 'by grab, I'll tell you! How'd you get all them cattle moved in here?'

'We had close to half of them here already. They're not all Rafters. There's a lot of small spreads got their stuff in here.'

'What connection has Rafter with these small outfits?'

'No connection at all. We just work together. In a common chore we pool our men.'

'Which outfits are workin' with you right now?'

'Star Cross, Gourd an' Vine, Lazy 3, Circle 10. And of course Jude Strump's Boxed K.'

I remembered something then. I remembered the night before, at that saloon in Gisela. There'd been a Jude there, and

66

Lovelee had dropped by to 'visit Jude's mother'. I considered that careful. 'This Strump,' I said. 'Does he wear a black patch? Has he got a sick relation?'

I felt kind of mean about asking that last until I noticed the way big Drumm was eyeing me. He rolled the cigar stump across his mouth. After a while he nodded.

'What iron does he use? Where's his outfit located?'

'He's up by the Gallups near the Pleasant Valley road.' There was a deal of speculation got afoot in Drumm's stare.

I said, 'Didn't Bluff tell you fellers to stay out of here?'

'That was yesterday.' Drumm grinned.

'What's different today?'

Drumm played cautious. He didn't say anything. I said, 'It looks to me like you're tryin' to start trouble. Leavin' Bluff clean out of it you've got no right here. This is Hack Sloan's Brad and Dash range.'

'It was,' Drumm said. He eyed his cigar stump and pitched it away. 'It was,' he said, 'but Hack ain't usin' it. Hack Sloan ain't around this country no more."

'What do you know about that?'

'Not as much as I'd like to, But I'll tell you this much—Hack Sloan was our friend. I think that's why they killed him.'

'Who said he was dead?'

Drumm grinned without mirth. 'Does a man

go off an' leave this kinda place?'

'That don't necessarily mean he's dead.'

'What does it mean then?' Drumm looked at me scornful. 'I guess you don't know much about things here. This here basin is the only good range that ain't packin' Bluff's brand— it's better range, even, than Bluff's got himself. Sloan already had this before Bluff come in. Bluff made him some offers but Hack wasn't sellin'; he liked this place. Then he begun havin' troubles. Hard luck got to campin' on the trail of Hack's men. A horse throwed one of 'em—broke his neck, a guy that had spent half his life stompin' rough ones. Another feller got drug—got his foot hung up in a stirrup, they tell me. A couple more gents stepped into a bullet. The rest up an' quit the country. Rustlers moved in then an' run off Hack's cattle, all the stuff he could market. An' now Hack's gone. If he ain't dead where is he?'

'That'll take some provin'.'

'That's what they sent you up here for, ain't it?'

We looked at each other. Drumm dug out a plug of black tobacco, bit off a chew and tramped into the house.

I followed him through Sloan's dusty rooms. You could see plain enough there hadn't been nobody living there. Drumm went out the back door and I went after him.

There was a man on the ground underneath

68

a blanket. Drumm pulled it off.

I didn't look long at Jim Varlance's face. His eyes stuck out and he wasn't pretty He'd been shot through the head. From behind. With a gun.

'You better start movin' them cattle out of here,' I said.

Drumm looked over the hills and said nothing.

Hard looks run off him just like rain.

Rain, I thought, and stared at the ground in considerable surprise. It hadn't rained here. It hadn't rained a drop.

I looked back at Drumm. 'These cattle,' I said, 'are a threat to the peace. You might's well wave a red flag in Bluff's face. Get 'em rounded up. Get 'em started out of here.'

Drumm kept on chewing. He run his glance over Varlance again like he was telling dead Jim not to pay no mind to me.

'There ain't goin' to be no range war round here!' I said, getting riled.

Drumm folded the blanket. 'I'm considerable relieved to hear you say that. There's been folks around that've had other notions. I expect they ain't never met no Rangers.'

I could feel the heat burn into my face. I was so mad I could feel my knees shake. I looked down at Varlance and damn near choked. One of his boot soles was cracked clean across.

69

CHAPTER EIGHT

All kind of wild thoughts rushed through my head. That boot sure gummed things up for fair. I'd of swore it was the boot that had left that track on the Straddle Bug porch.

I scowled at the ground all around me careful. 'Who made all them tracks?'

'Reckon you kin guess about as good as I can.'

'You mean them tracks was here when you found him?'

'Most of 'em was. We might of made a few.'

'You talk mighty sure.'

'We struck a few matches. You'll find 'em around. We could see plain enough there was plenty of tracks.'

'Too bad,' I said, 'you had to add your hoof marks. It would take a Injun to read sign now.'

'Sorry,' Drumm said. 'A feller can't think of everythin'. I was some disturbed findin' Jim Varlance like that.'

'How come it didn't rain around here last night?'

'I don't know,' Drumm said. 'I ain't been informed.'

'Was them horse tracks there?' I looked at him black like.

'They was jest like you see 'em. I been campin' right here ever sinst we found—'

70

'"We!"' I said. 'I thought you told me *you* found him!'

'I did. But Moran was with me.'

'All right,' I said. 'Let's have the rest of it. Did you hear the shot?'

'We didn't hear nothin'. I'd been makin' the rounds. I figured we might have trouble with Bluff an' I allowed to make sure all the boys was awake. I got back about nine—'

'Did you look at your watch?'

'I don't pack no watch.'

'Then how do you place the time so close?'

Drumm answered like his patience was wearing thin. 'I ain't got no proof for none of this stuff—you kin take it or leave it. I don't need no clock to know what time it is.'

'All right,' I said. 'You got here round nine. Who else was here?'

'I didn't see nobody, includin' Jim. I put up my horse in that corral over there. I went round an' set on the porch a while, smokin'. Moran rode up. He asked if I'd seen anything of Jim, who had gone down to Tailpiece after supplies. He'd been gone quite a while. I got kind of uneasy. I decided to look round.'

'You thought mebba Varlance was lost?'

'I thought mebbe he'd been jumped by some of them Straddle Bugs. Bluff hires a tough crew an' there was bad blood between us. Jim kind of had notions about marryin' Bluff's girl. That was three-four months ago. They used to slip off an' meet theirselfs

71

sometimes. A couple months ago Bluff found out about it. He come over to the Rafter an' damn near set the place afire with his language. You'd of thought Jim had— Anyway, Jim had left here last evenin' around six-thirty, or mebbe it was six, an' when it got to shovin' ten an' he hadn't come back we decided to look. I come through the house here to get me a horse. I come out that door like we done just now an' started for the corral. I'd—'

'Did you stumble over him?'

'No. I seen somethin' dark here an' struck a match. Cancho Moran was out front with his horse. I called him.'

'Call him now,' I said, and Drumm done it.

Moran come through the house the same way that we had. I could see how it might of been like that. I said, 'What happened then?'

'I sent Moran after you.'

'Yeah,' I said, and took another look at Jim Varlance's boots.

The way the times was, I couldn't see how Varlance could of packed Bluff home and still be back here by ten. He'd gone off himself between six and six-thirty. Of course he might never have gone down to Tailpiece at all. Bluff had left his crowd around seven o'clock. Bluff could of got here around seven-thirty, or Varlance and him might of met someplace else. Bluff had been stabbed from behind which made it look like stalking. Stalking takes

72

time. Then, if Bluff had been killed by Varlance, he'd of had to been packed from here or somewheres around here clean over to the Straddle Bug. Varlance, then, would of had to get back here in a pretty big rush to of been found dead here himself by ten.

I didn't think he could. Besides, where was the blood he must of got on his clothes packing Bluff around that way? There was dust on Jim's clothes but I didn't see no blood; and suddenly it struck me that was damn peculiar. He was laying with his head kind of turned to one side. The blood should of spread that way but it hadn't. Like Bluff's, Varlance's blood had run uphill.

*   *   *

'What time do you figure your boss was killed?'

'Well,' Drumm declared, 'I been thinkin' about that. I would say he was shot between seven an' seven-thirty. I'm just guessing, of course, but none of our crowd was around here then.'

'Convenient,' I said. 'Mighty convenient.'

Moran kind of grinned. It didn't improve my temper none.

'You don't have to believe me,' Drumm said.

'What'd you do after Moran rode off?'

'I went over an' set on that bench.' Drumm

pointed. 'Right there on that bench against the house. I set there an' smoked up a couple cigars. I expect you can find the butts around someplace.'

I didn't doubt that. I didn't guess no dead man would bother him much.

'You got anything else on your mind I should know about?'

Drumm looked at Varlance. I considered him myself. I wondered if he had been packed in like Bluff had.

'You say he went after grub. What'd he do with it?'

Drumm shrugged.

'It ain't in the house,' I said.

'I didn't see no sign of it.'

So he'd gone after grub and hadn't got back with it. Maybe they'd nailed him at Tailpiece. I thought, by grab, I had ought to go down there.

'Who do you reckon killed him?' I said.

Drumm didn't answer but it was plain what he thought. He was sure in his own mind it was someone from Straddle Bug.

I expect, in his place, I'd of thought so, too. I did fiddle round for a bit along them lines. But it seemed too simple, like we was intended to think that. I mean with all of this range trouble floating round, a feller would naturally jump to that notion. But it seemed too pat, too blamed ready to hand. And it didn't seem likely that both these outfits would play that

74

kind of game. Bushwhackers is usually low-calibered specimens, though not by any means always. A range feud brings out the worst in a man, as who should know better than me who'd been in some.

So I couldn't rule it out, but it seemed to me like the killer in this case might be somebody else, some party who wanted to get a war started. There is fellers like that in every man's country, chicken-livered worms that makes fat off a carcass.

'What'll you do now that Jim's gone?' I said.

'I'll be around. I'll take care of his interests.'

The look of his eyes said a heap more than that. They had the same kind of look I had seen in young Dandy's.

'Some guy,' I said, 'might like you to do that.'

Drumm hid his thoughts but his face didn't change any.

I said, 'The Law has arrived in this country, Drumm. You had better remember it. Give me half a chance an' I'll unravel this thing. I'll put the blame where the blame belongs and see that the guilty is brought to justice. Never mind no remarks now. You get them cattle out of here, that's your job.'

Drumm stared at the hills quite a while without speaking. 'If we pull these cattle out,' he said finally, 'what's to stop Bluff from shovin' his in?'

'I'll take care of that.'

75

'You better,' Drumm said, and jerked a nod at Moran. 'Go ahead, Cancho. Get the boys an' start driftin' 'em.' His eyes come back cold and hard to mine. 'If you're sellin' us out—'

He stopped right there with his head cocked, listening. I heard it, too. There was a horse around somewheres coming through the brush.

I seen Moran and Drumm swapping looks. Moran ducked into the house. We could hear his boots pounding toward the front. Then his voice come back: 'Hell, it's only the doc.' and we let our breaths out.

'Send him around,' I said, and presently the doc come around the house on his horse, a wizzled-up apron-faced roan with spavins. He unbent enough to give us a nod and finally groaned himself out of the saddle and hunkered down with his bag beside Jim's body.

'I'm Waggoner,' I said. 'One of Mossman's Rangers. Near as you can put it, I'd like to know what time this feller was killed?'

He didn't look up. He didn't say nothing, neither.

Drumm jerked a nod toward a clump of box elders. I went over there with him and scowled at some horse tracks. A kid could of read that sign with his eyes shut; it hadn't been scuffed like the tracks around Jim's body. Some horse had stood there an uncommon long while.

'Well,' I said, 'what about it?'

Drumm crossed his arms and looked sour

without speaking.

I took another look without improving my knowledge. I said, 'Do you happen to know anything about his relations? We ought to be gettin' them word about this.'

'Jim hadn't no relations but me.'

I was a little surprised. I hadn't thought of Drumm as being related to Varlance. 'Didn't know you was any kin to him,' I said.

'I'm not, the way you mean. He didn't have any kinfolks. I'm all that he had. I'm his sole beneficiary.'

It might of been the way Drumm said it. Or maybe something in his look. But I didn't like the way things was shaping.

Drumm seen I didn't. He nodded grimly. 'It's true enough, Waggoner. Jim give me everything—every last thing he might die possessed of. All his goods, all his chattels. You can check with Moran. You can ask the whole outfit.'

'When did this happen'?' I said.

'Yesterday. In Greenback. Right after Bluff warned us out of the basin. Jim allowed we had better get ready for trouble. We each drawed a deed in favor of the other. Not that I had much to deed Jim, but that's the way he wanted it.'

'You sure done it mighty convenient!'

'Well, that was the way it was.'

'Where was you last night between seven an' nine?'

'Right where I said I was. Makin' the rounds. Makin' sure our boys was all up an' ready for any damn thing Harry Bluff might try.'

'Well,' I said, 'I hope you can prove it.'

'I can prove it, all right. Mebbe not where I was every minute, but I can damn well prove I was makin' the rounds.'

'What time last night do you reckon Bluff died?'

Drumm's expression froze solid. His eyes hid away everything he was thinking. He said through his teeth, 'That would be plumb funny if there was any truth in it.'

'Then you better get ready to laugh,' I said. 'He was found on his porch dark an' late last night with a bonehandled knife buried back of his wish-bone.'

Drumm didn't laugh. His face stayed blank as a bullet. 'I thought Harry Bluff was goin' over to Roblero's,' he said, and his eyes never left my face.

'If you thought that,' I said, 'what the hell was eatin' you? Why was you postin' all your men for trouble?'

'That's why,' Drumm said. 'Because he was goin' to Roblero's. Harry's full of them tricks. Sly little dodges to ketch a guy nappin'.'

He twitched his shoulders and went over to the doc. I went after him. The doc got up and brushed off his knees. He give us a owlish stare through his glasses. 'It would take an autopsy to say for sure, but I would say Jim quit breathing between seven and seven-thirty.'

I stared at Drumm. Drumm was staring at me.

'When was Harry Bluff killed?' I asked the doc.

'About a half-hour later.'

Drumm wiped the backs of his hands on his pants. There was a damn funny look peering out of his stare. He started to turn away and then swung round and come back.

'I'm goin' to move out them cattle like I said I would, but you'll see more gun smoke before this is done with.'

I caught his arm. 'What's the meanin' of that?'

'You'll see some,' he grumbled; and then he give me a grin. 'You're a Ranger,' he said. 'Try rangin' on that.'

He tossed me a crumpled-up square of stained cambric.

'That stuff's blood,' he pointed out. 'Them dark spots on it.'

He didn't have to confide whose blood it was. He didn't have to say it was a woman's handkerchief, nor what was the name of the woman it belonged to. The lavender perfume told me that.

CHAPTER NINE

My heart was like water.

I could see her plain with a smoking pistol and her pretty face all swole with tears. I could see her that plain it made me sick. I tried to think if I could hide that thing in the palm of my hand. I tried to think how I could buy off the doc and what I could do that would make Drumm feel good, but I knew all the time there was nothing I could do.

Then I thought of the cracked-sole boots that was on Varlance's feet. I grabbed a deep breath and tried to yank myself together.

'Whereabouts did you find that, Drumm?' I said. I tried to sound unfussed, but my words come out like they was squeezed through a wringer.

'On the ground,' Drumm said. 'Right beside Jim's body.' He looked at me steadily like he seen I had recognized the thing. 'It's a woman's handkerchief,' he added, pointedly.

I nodded, casual like. 'Well, I suppose it was there before Jim was,' I said, and seen right away that nobody believed it. 'Anyways,' I said, 'it don't prove nothin'. The woman prob'ly heard the shot. She was rushin' up an' found Jim dyin'. She tried to—'

'Sure,' Drumm grinned, 'she tried all right. I reckon she tried to shove the brains back in him.' He spat out an amber stream at the bushes. 'They learn you all that at the Ranger school?'

'All right!' I snarled. 'What do *you* think she done?'

'I think she killed him.'

The doc got pale around the gills and started sweating. 'I think—uh, perhaps—I've got to get back to town. If you will favor me, Drumm, by fetchin'—'

'Sure,' Drumm said. He kept his eyes on me.

The doc looked relieved and got out of there pronto. Moran come back, through the house like before.

'Reckon I don't have to name no names,' Drumm said softly. 'So you don't think she done it, eh?'

'Of course she never done it! That was a fine thing to spill in front of that pill-pounder! Why would she kill him? She was sweet on him, wasn't she?'

'Her ol' man wasn't sweet on him.'

'That ain't no reason—' I looked at Drumm blankly. 'Was Driver around when Bluff kicked up that deadline?'

'They was all there,' Drumm said. 'Driver and that wolf-pack crew he hires. The ol' man, the girl—they was all there but Dandy.'

'Drumm,' I said, 'Jim must of weighed pretty close to two hundred. No woman could have got him up onto a horse—'

'On a horse!' Drumm said. 'What the hell are you talkin' of? She didn't have to get him up on no horse.'

'Then how did she get him here? She sure didn't pack him! An' he wasn't killed here.'

'What the hell you been smokin'?'

I waved that away. 'Have you looked at that wound? Did you ever see blood flow uphill before? There ain't but one way for a man to figure this. Jim was killed someplace else an' packed in here dead.'

It did my heart good to tell that guy something.

Drumm looked at me like he couldn't believe it. 'Don't they learn you Rangers how t' read signs?'

I begun to feel cold down around my belt line.

Drumm shook his head mournful and spit out his tobacco. 'You remember them tracks you seen by the elders? That's where she waited. When she heard him comin' she went into them cottonwoods, I figure they talked some—argued, mebbe. Then he started for the horse pen an' that's when she plugged him.'

The hell of it was a lot of folks might believe that. If he got to passing such ideas around they was due to get swallowed by a whole lot of people.

Like he read my mind Drumm nodded at me owlish like. 'When she fired off her gun Jim fell outen his saddle. See that scuffed place yonder like where somethin' was dragged? Somethin' was Jim Varlance. He'd hung a foot in the stirrup. His horse come apart an' took off for Montana. The girl took out after him; it was her horse an' his horse that made them tracks. Right there's where she stopped him. Look at these.' Drumm pointed. 'There's where she got his foot outen the stirrup. Them's the marks of her knees where she bent down beside him; she figured to make sure he wouldn't be doin' no talkin'. There's where she swung up on her bronc again, an' right there,' he pointed 'is where she rode out of here. You can foller that sign plumb to Bluff's ranch, I'm bettin'.'

It didn't make no difference if he believed it or not. If he ever got up and told that to a jury—

The short hair on my neck started to crawl. Drumm's words opened up a whole pile of things that had been rubbing chafed spots into my thinking. No wonder she'd looked scairt. I have knowed plenty of men that couldn't of stood up to that stuff. And all the time I'd been pounding her with questions these was the pictures she'd had chousing through her head. Not that I believed for one second she had done it, but there it was. I mean you couldn't get around it.

I went over to the cottonwoods and no one could of looked them over better than I did. I found tracks all right. It could of been just the way this guy Drumm told it.

I come back and went over the ground around Varlance.

There wasn't nothing there that could disprove him neither. And when the jury asked to see that bloodstained handkerchief, and got them to whiff of that lavender perfume—

'How you explainin' that blood on the handkerchief?' I said. There was enough cold sweat on my back to wash with.

'It explains itself. She had to wipe off her hands on something.'

'Did she have to throw it down right alongside his body?'

'She was probably excited. I don't guess she realized she had even let go of it. A woman don't think like a man. A woman's nature—' Drumm said, and broke off, reaching hipward.

Horsebackers were coming through the brush toward us. Three of them there was, and you could see the sun glinting off the barrels of their rifles.

The feller in the lead was Jude Strump, I reckoned; anyways, he was the black-patched jasper I had met at Gisela. The other two was punchers, the same breed of coyotes Bluff's Straddle Bug hired. They was gun-hung drifters that would do what they was told to do so long as they figured their boss could take care of them.

I seen the thin shine of Drumm's hard teeth. Black Patch nodded, not at me but at

Drumm. Then his eyes hit the corpse and his face kind of stiffened. While I watched, it broke up into a bunch of pleased creases round a mighty wide grin. 'Well, well!' he said. 'So they got Jim Varlance.'

Drumm said, 'I laughed too when I heard about Bluff.'

I looked from one to the other of them puzzled. Why was these fellers glaring like a couple of chained bobcats? It didn't make sense, them slinging that kind of talk. Wasn't this the Jude Strump that ranged his cattle with Rafter? If it was, why the leering over dead Jim's killing?

It was then I remembered that snatch of talk at Gisela when Black Patch and me had swapped bowkays with our teeth bared, and that guy saying, 'Don't waste your breath on the peckerneck, Jude. Bluff will know how to deal with him!'

Bluff! But that was right. He had said Bluff.

Which side of this thing was Jude Strump on, anyway?

I looked at the guy's twisted face and I wondered. 'Bluff!' He was glaring. 'What about Bluff?'

'Why, ain't you heard?' Drumm said real concerned like. 'Somebody shoved a knife in him last night. I would thought you'd of heard all about it by now.'

Black Patch raised the muzzle of his rifle. But Drumm's eyes didn't change none. They

85

was cold and contemptuous.

'By Gawd, if that's so,' Black Patch said, wild and reckless, 'there's due to be a pile of unwore clothes in your bunkhouse!'

'That's enough of that talk,' I said, and hauled out my smoke pole. 'Just tuck them lightnin' rods back where you got 'em.'

'Who ast you into this?' Black Patch growled.

'A rep for the governor ain't needin' no invite.'

'To hell with the gov'nor! We kin iron this out—'

'You mean,' Drumm said, 'like you "ironed out" Jim?'

'Why, you meechin' two-bit badman! I'll—'

There was no use wasting good breath on that guy. I put a shot across his saddle and he let go his rifle like you'd thought it had burnt him.

Drumm looked disgusted. Moran's teeth showed through his scraggle of whiskers. The two punchers was watching for signals.

Black Patch give me a dirty look.

'My name's Waggoner,' I said. 'Is yours Strump?'

'Sure it's Strump,' Drumm said. 'That's the great politician, *Mister* Jude Strump, what figures to wed himself into the Straddle Bug. Last week he was lickin' Jim Varlance's boots. Tomorrow—'

'You kin talk mighty brash while your

friend's got the drop,' Strump snarled.

'Latch your lip,' I said. 'An' that applies to you, too, Drumm. I'll do the talkin'. What was you figurin' to do around here, Strump?'

'As a matter of fact, we was huntin' a horse.'

'Well, well!' I said, like the way he had said it. 'This is sure stackin' up to be quite a horse country. What kind of a horse did you lose?'

'I kin get him back without help from you!'

'That bein' the case you can romp right along then. Make a noise with your gut hooks an' get on your way.' Then another idea changed my mind and I said, 'Just a minute! I guess you know most of the folks that live round here. Take a look at that dead gent— take a good look, Strump, he ain't goin' to bite you. Would you swear that guy's Varlance?'

Strump's face said he thought I was loco.

'Take a good look,' I said, and he finally done it. I seen his shape stiffen. His mouth come open. That was what I was waiting for.

'Well,' I said. 'Is it Varlance or ain't it?'

He never said a word. He hauled up his jaw and backed his horse and wheeled him around like he had urgent business.

'Ain't you goin' to pick up your artillery?' I asked.

But Strump was gone. His two punchers swore and took off after him.

*　　*　　*

87

When the dust had settled I said to Drumm, 'Where did Jim Varlance get them boots?'

'I been wonderin',' Drumm said. He looked at me funny. 'Come here a minute.'

I followed him over to Jim's dead body. Drumm flipped a hand, indicating the scenery. 'You've seen this ground. You've looked it all over. Did you notice any tracks from that cracked-sole boot?'

I shook my head.

'Did you look for any?'

'I looked,' I said.

'Well, I looked, too, an' I didn't see none. I been camped right here ever sinst we found him. I ain't found no tracks that would match that boot. Does that mean anything to a Ranger, Wagonner?'

'Yeah,' I said, 'but it ain't conclusive. They coulda been rubbed out.'

'I thought of that,' Drumm said. 'It's too unlikely. This killer had to do his work in the dark; he couldn't of been sure he'd got 'em all.'

'Well?'

'All right. Look here.' He lifted Jim's foot and pulled off the boot. 'Take a look at that ankle,' Drumm's eyes met mine. 'Now tell me he wasn't dragged.'

'He's been dragged, all right.'

'Now look at the boot. How come there ain't no marks like that on it?'

'Suppose you tell me.'

'I'll tell you. I'll tell you them ain't his boots. Them boots was put on him after they killed him.'

CHAPTER TEN

I thought about that all the way back to Straddle Bug. I thought about a lot of things making that trip. I wondered if a guy could take the doc's word on the subject of when Bluff and Varlance had died. I didn't know that doc; I didn't know what his rep was or if his opinion could be influenced by cash.

I didn't like the thought of Jim Varlance dying first. I didn't like anything about this business.

Tom Driver was at the Bluff's corral when I got there. Strump was just coming out of the house. The kind of look he give me wouldn't of softened no water. He got up into his saddle, scowling.

'Driver,' I said, 'did you get that word passed around like I told you?'

'Western Union ain't payin' my wages.'

'There's a saw about wages you had better cull over. Where's the kid?'

Driver give me a shrug and, about that time, I seen the kid myself. He come out of the house and went off toward the cook shack.

I pulled the gear off my horse and penned

89

him. I picked up my pack and set it careful on the pole. I hung my bridle on the horn. On top I put the blanket, hair side up, to dry. And while I was doing it I done some thinking.

I was starting for the house to palaver with Lovelee when something I heard Strump say turned me round. I went up to him.

'What was that?' I said.

He scowled down at me, sullen. He was careful to keep his hands where I could see them. He said with a glower, 'I guess you heard me.'

'I guess I did, too. I just wondered if you had enough gall to repeat it. Since you're so damn smart, Strump, mebbe you can tell me who killed these fellers.'

'You bet I kin tell yer. Drumm, that's who! He's been layin' fer Harry ever sinst Harry caught him bustin' hell outa Sloan.'

'Where'd you get that notion?'

'I didn't figure you'd believe me.'

'I might if I knowed more about it,' I said. 'When did this happen?'

'It was a couple of days before Sloan turned up missin'.'

'An' you think Drumm killed Bluff to keep him from tellin' that?'

'It's a pretty good reason. Bluff sees him beatin' up on the ol' gent an' a couple days after that Sloan disappears. I'd call it plenty of reason if I'd been caught that way.'

'An' about how long would you say Hack's

90

been missin'?'

I tried to slip it in quick like, but Strump twisted round and shot a look at Tom Driver.

'I'm askin' Strump,' I said, and seen Driver's eyes glint. He shut his mouth. Strump shut his mouth, too.

'Well,' I said, 'let's put it this way. Would you reckon he'd been gone for as long as five weeks?'

Strump shifted his seat around in the saddle. The way he wrinkled his face didn't help out his looks none. He sure didn't want to be pinned down to nothing. 'I guess so,' he grumbled. 'I reckon that would cover it.'

'Then you'd say he disappeared about the time Bluff come back from Gisela—that right?'

'Huh! Bluff! From Gisela?' Strump's look jumped to Driver and come back at me ugly. 'What the hell you tryin' to ring in on me? Bluff went t' Willcox.'

'He means the kid,' Driver grunted. 'Young Dandy.'

'Why the hell didn't he say the kid then an' not hand me—'

'I been tryin',' I said, 'to get this straight in my mind. If Drumm killed Bluff to keep Bluff from talkin'—'

'I told you. Bluff caught him tryin' to beat ol' Sloan. Then Sloan turns up missin—'

'An' to keep Bluff from talkin', Drumm fiddles around for five long weeks an' then

91

flogs a bronc over here an' shoves a knife into Bluff. Mebbe,' I said, 'some guys would believe that. But if I was doin' it, I'd say the time to of done it was right when Bluff caught him.'

Strump growled, 'Sloan hadn't disappeared then.'

'But accordin' to you he was missed two days later. Then Drumm sets around for five weeks—'

'Why, damn you,' snarled Strump, 'do you think he was goin' clean t' Willcox t' kill him?'

'Where does Willcox come into it?'

'Bluff only got back from Willcox last night! He's been down there buyin' him another bunch of cattle.' Strump gathered his reins and looked down at me scornful. 'I can't figure how you ever got in the Rangers. You don't look t' know half as much as my horse.'

*   *   *

I didn't argue it with him. I let him ride off feeling full of importance, then I went in the house to have my confab with Lovelee. But she wasn't around or, if she was, I didn't see her. I didn't see the kid around anyplace neither, and when I got back outside Tom Driver was gone.

Driver, I reckoned, had chores to take care of. But I couldn't see the kid trying to make himself useful. I suspected he was round but was keeping out of sight.

Then I remembered I'd seen him heading for the cook shack. Thinking of the cook shack reminded me I was hungry so I dragged my spurs on over there. There wasn't nobody around but there was some warmed-over stuff on the back of the stove.

I got me a plate and shoveled some on it. The coffee was strong enough to carry double but I poured me out a big cup of it and went and set down where I could watch both the doors and keep an eye on the window. Not that I was nervous. I was just being careful.

Nobody showed while I was feeding my face and it kind of struck me funny where the hell all the crew was. Naturally the most of them would be riding the range but it looked like there had ought to be a couple of them round.

I got to thinking of Lovelee about that time and forgot them. How was a feller to ask that girl what she had been doing over at Sloan's ranch last night? I got to stewing over that and set there a considerable while longer than I aimed to. She sure was in one hell of a spot.

I finished with my eating and rolled me up a smoke. I seen dang well I ought to talk to her pronto. I ought to find out about that handkerchief. I'd ought to find out about Jim Varlance's boots and how come he'd got them cracked-sole ones on. I'd ought to get her account of what she'd been doing there, what she had seen and all about it.

I half got up and then I set down again. I

93

could talk with her later. I reckoned she was probably in her room laying down. Like enough she was crying. She'd got plenty to make her cry, all right, if any of that stuff Drumm had said was true. Not that I figured very much of it was, but it sure looked a heap like she had been round there. If she had she must of seen something I ought to know.

Of one thing I felt pretty sure. These killings wasn't sprung from no range feud. Jim Varlance wasn't the kind to stab a guy in the back. Besides, he couldn't of killed Bluff, he'd been dead before Bluff was. He had, anyway, if I could believe that doc.

I went over again the things I'd found out so far. According to the evidence Varlance had got himself killed between seven and seven-thirty, by parties unknown. Then Bluff, the big boss of the Straddle Bugs, turns up on his porch with a knife in his back. He'd been killed about a half an hour later.

This far, anyone would have said this was just the old trouble between two rival outfits, the natural upshot of the bad blood between them. But what about that cracked-sole boot that had left its track beside Bluff's body and then turned up on dead Jim Varlance? Them boots throwed the whole thing hell west and crooked. Drumm had made no mistake when he told me them boots was put onto his boss after Varlance was dead. And what about Sloan? Where the devil was he at?

The more I fussed and fumed at this business the more it looked like Sloan was the start of it. Everything stemmed from Sloan's disappearance. The kid come back from a trip to Gisela. The kid's old man took a jaunt down to Willcox to buy him more cattle, probably to put on Sloan's range. The girl baked a pie which she had aimed to give Sloan, which she had taken, in fact, to Sloan's house and there left it. But it hadn't been ate. The old man hadn't touched it. I should of looked for that pie when I'd been there this morning.

Besides these things, there was Strump's great tale about Bluff and Drumm, which might be true but which, also, might not be. There was, likewise, that deed-swapping deal of Drumm and Jim Varlance, and there was all them things Drumm had said about Lovelee.

The guy back of this wasn't no damn fool.

On that thought I stubbed out my smoke. I got up and was heading for the outside again when Driver barged in looking hell-bent for trouble.

'You seen Lovelee?' I said, and he looked at me black like. He went out through the back really heating his axles.

I stared after him wondering what had got in his craw. Then I reached for the knife I had pulled out of Bluff and that was when I got worried really.

The knife was gone. I didn't have it no more. I had put it in my belt but it wasn't there now. It was loose, like the killer, free to strike again.

CHAPTER ELEVEN

I hunted the yard and I didn't find it.

Driver came out of the saddle shed just as I was wondering where to look next. 'Where's Dandy?' I said, wondering if maybe the kid might of seen it.

'Gone off t' town,' Driver growled without stopping. He sure was in a whittle-whanging mood. I didn't know what had got him so riled and I hadn't no time right then to consider it. Right then all my thoughts was on that knife. A fine fool I'd look at that inquest without it.

I grabbed up my rope and climbed into the corral. I hadn't knowed I was tired till I made two throws without snagging nothing but a ropeful of air. By that time them horses were stirred up right. They was ducking and weaving and snorting and blowing, but the next time I seen my roan bolt past I'd throwed my rope and he stepped right into it.

All the time I was saddling up I kept trying to figure where that knife had got to. It could make a heap of difference. If the killer had got his claws on it I might better be hunting a needle in a haystack. But if the killer hadn't got it, a heap of close looking might yet turn it

96

up and save me their sneers.

I aimed to look.

And done it, too. I looked all the way to Sloan's ranch buildings and all around Sloan's house and yard, working over the ground I had covered that morning so near as memory would let me. I got rid of a lot of time in that fashion and picked up more or less knowledge of the country, but I didn't pick up that dadburned knife.

It looked a pretty safe bet it had been found already.

Cattle was a dust south and east of Sloan's, from which it looked like Drumm might of talked with a honest tongue. He was anyways getting them started out of there and, not wanting to get his mind off the business, I decided to have me a look at Tailpiece, Del Widney's Saloon at Tin Can Springs, where Jim Varlance had gone for supplies. It also happened to be near Bear Head Mountain, which, if I'd been told right, was the scene of the kid's hunting for a horse.

Drumm hadn't talked like it was very far off when he'd told me about Jim Varlance going there. It was someplace south and east of me and Bear Head Mountain was pretty much likely to be one of them four tall peaks off that way; one of them did kind of look like a bear's head if you didn't know what a bear's head looked like.

Names, I've found, is mostly that way, like

calling a real fat feller Slim or calling a long tall jasper Half Pint.

Alongside the basin this was mighty poor country. It was a tawny, bleached yellow kind of a land without no trees, but scrubby mesquites which was pretty well clipped of their leaves by cows trying to get something to pad out their ribs with. Ocotillo was scattered all through this region and considerable cholla that was overgrowed and colored like a bunch of dirty sheep. There wasn't no sign of grass whatever. It was a burnt-out country, the natural home of coyotes and buzzards and, as I cut a wide skirt to keep out of hail of Drumm's swearing riders, I felt right-down sorry for them bellering cattle I was making the Rafter pull out of Sloan's grass.

Some time after I'd put them behind I seen a guy a good piece south which seemed to be angling for the same peaks I was. He was too far off for me to make out much. He was riding a dun and seemed mighty anxious to keep out of sight. The country down there looked more cut up than this was, a kind of a badlands criss-crossed with gullies and barren mesas.

Pretty soon I was skirting some arroyos myself, and then I was dropping down into a canyon whose side walls was rust-colored jumbles of rock, weathered and splintered and gnarled with time. I went careful down there. Its floor was strewed with boulders and juniper, and jack rabbits seemed to be jumping all over. It was a place I was glad to get out of. It was built too much like a trap for my fancy and it like to of put my eyes out keeping them all the time peeled for the fugitive shine of some lurking rifle.

I begun to wonder if I'd missed Tailpiece and if maybe I hadn't better be turning back. It wouldn't look extry good for my ability if something broke loose while I was doing this rambling. I said to the forward-cocked ears of my horse, 'What the hell have you done with that dadburned saloon?'

And then we seen it.

We come out of a draw and there it was, brush sides with a tarp stretched across a ridgepole and a kind of ramada throwed up out front. There was brush piled deep on the top of the cross-joists and, in this shade, there was two-three kegs and a couple of benches. Some flies was doing a lively buzzing but there wasn't no human critters in sight.

Off to one side, by the springs themselves, was some piles of tin cans and broken bottles. A mesquite stake corral was just beyond with four or five sorry-looking broomtails in it. Anchored to the flat brush roof of the store was a ten-foot sign which said *Saloon.*

One bony bronc was ground-hitched by the side of it, a dun like the one I had seen cutting south.

*   *   *

There is a kind of etiquette that most gents observes when they come in sight of another man's buildings. On such occasions politeness is measured by the amount of noise a feller puts in his greeting.

I fetched up my hog-calling voice and yelled howdy. And I kept where I was in plain sight in the saddle till a gent stuck his head out the door of the 'store'.

'Lookin' for somethin'?' this specimen says.

'I'd be pleasured to swap a few words with Del Widney.'

'Start swappin' 'em then—I'm Widney,' he said in a voice that plumb run over with welcome.

'Kinda hot up here in the saddle,' I told him.

That heat didn't look to be thawing him out much. His shoe-button eyes combed me over plumb hostile. 'Wal, git down,' he said, like it might of hurt him. 'I been lookin' fer you t' come pokin' around. You're that feller that's stayin' at the Straddle Bug, ain'tcha?'

'Yeah. The name's Waggoner.'

'I don't keer about that. What do you want here?'

'Do I have to want somethin'?'

'I ain't got nothin' here that would interest no Ranger.'

'Well,' I said, 'I could do with a drink. Mebbe your friend would like to come out an'

100

join us.'

Widney's look didn't warm none. He kept one hand near the butt of his pistol while a guy come reluctant like out of the store and edged through the shade with his stare pale and watchful. He set himself down on one of the benches and give me a grudging nod. He was a gray-haired gent with the look of a mouse.

I said to Del Widney, 'Varlance stop here last night?'

He give it some thought and finally nodded.

'What time?' I said.

'I dunno's I remember.'

But he remembered all right. Then the old man looked up and said through his whiskers, 'He left fer Sloan's ranch about a quarter till seven.'

'Buy any groceries?' I said to Widney.

'A few. A little tinned stuff. Bought some flour an' salt.'

'Young Bluff come by any time last night?'

'He stopped in.' Widney scowled. 'About nine-thirty.'

'Was he huntin' a horse?'

Widney shrugged. 'He didn't mention.'

'How long was he here?'

Widney's scowl turned darker. 'Look,' he said, 'I try t' live with my neighbors. I'm runnin' a business—I don't try to run theirs.'

'That's a Christian spirit that does you credit. How long was he here?'

Widney scowled a long while. I kept on

waiting.

'I don't know what you expect t' find out,' Widney finally grumbled, 'but I don't think I keer t' answer that question. That Straddle Bug outfit is best left alone. It don't pay a man good t' git them down on him. I wouldn't want them t' think—' He scowled again and quit talking. 'Then he said, half defiant, 'You wouldn't neither, if you was standin' in my boots.'

'The kid says,' I told him, 'he was here quite a spell. You don't have to tell me nothin' you don't want to, but young Bluff might reckon you was doin' him a favor did you happen to remember what time he pulled out of here.'

'In that case,' said Widney, 'I don't mind sayin'. Matter of fact, he was here about a hour an' a quarter. We played cards mostly. We had a few drinks—'

'He was in the habit of droppin' around for a few hands of cards, was he?'

'Well, he hadn't been, no. Only just recent. His old man never had no use fer the pasteboards, never would stand t' hev a card in the house—nor in his bunkhouse, neither. Reg'lar teetotaler, too. Some of his crew used t' drop round sometimes but he'd of fired 'em, I reckon, if he ever had ketched 'em. Here the las' month or so the kid taken t' comin'. Expect he figgers he's weaned. Might be he is he put likker away jest like it was water.'

'Yeah. About last night,' I reminded him.

102

'Did the kid say anythin' about goin' to Roblero's?'

'Said he guessed he would hev t' look in fer a minute. He didn't seem none perked up about it. Gab, gab, gab. He says it makes his guts ache. He quit my place here about ten-thirty. How I happen t' know is I wound up the clock right after he left.'

So there was the truth of the kid's hunt for horses.

I eyed the old man. Something about that old codger struck me. And then I remembered. I had seen this feller at Gisela. He had been with Jude Strump. He'd been the one guy with Jude that hadn't done any talking.

He wasn't doing much now.

I said, 'You ever met up with this feller Drumm?'

'Cal Drumm?' he said. 'I usually make out to know him when I see him, mostly.'

He picked up a stick and got out his knife. He stropped it a couple of times on a boot sole. He looked the stick all over and cut off the end of it. He held it up to his eye. He took a long squint and nodded.

'Yep. I usually make out to know Mister Drumm when I see him.'

He sharpened his knife again and started whittling.

I considered him a while. It didn't look like neither of them had much to add in the way of conversation. 'How long have you knowed him?'

'Knowed him most of his life,' he said.

'If I could get him to talk could I believe what he told me?'

He looked up then, quit whittling. He looked kind of funny. 'You better ask somebody else about Drumm. Don't ask a man's friends a thing like that, boy.'

'You're a friend of his, are you? Ever worked for him, have you?'

'Worked for him!' Widney said, and slapped his thigh. He squinted his eyes and give a loud laugh. 'This guy's ol' Les Trumbet, Cal Drumm's right hand! Didn't you know Les was down in Drumm's books as range boss?'

I reckon I gawped like a common fool. But honest, that guy didn't look like no range boss. He looked like a busted-down booze-guzzling bum. With his watery stare and ragged mustache, with his uncut stubble of gray-streaked whiskers, he looked like the last thing you'd want on your payroll. Why, I wouldn't of hired him to hold my horse!

Widney seen my look. He sniggered. Color climbed into the old man's cheeks but he showed no offense. He looked up at me tiredly.

'I know I ain't much good,' Les Trumbet said. 'Drumm give me that job outa Christian kindness. He knowed I wouldn't be round much longer. He—he kinda wanted me to feel like I belonged round here.'

I looked at Del Widney but I wasn't seeing him. I was seeing this old guy with Strump at Gisela. I was recalling the feverish look of his stare as he'd gulped down his drink and trailed after them others.

There was something about this that I wasn't getting.

'If you're wagon boss for Drumm,' I said, 'how does it happen that I seen—'

The look of his eyes suddenly reached out and stopped me. There was fear in that look. It was right close to panic.

There ain't no excuse for the way I done him. A kid in rompers would of had more sense than to stand there gawping the way I done. Widney looked at me and then he gawped, too.

Old Les give a shaky laugh and said sick like, 'Did you find that knife you was huntin' for, son?'

I guess I stared harder. I plain couldn't help it.

I remembered too late I was Burt Mossman's deputy. I was here to find out things, not give them away.

The old man looked like I had cooked his goose but he said one more thing. He said, 'I— I seen you drop it. That was how I knowed.'

'I don't guess you noticed who picked it up?'

Trumbet shook his head, 'I'm too old a man to get mixed up in this feudin'.'

He went back to his whittling and I wondered again what he'd been doing at Gisela with a feller his boss liked no better than poison. I wondered why he hadn't wanted Widney to know it. I wondered, but my wondering fetched up no answers.

The old man put down his stick and got onto his feet. He put the knife in his belt and went over to his horse and got into the saddle. He set there a minute looking dubious and nervous. He cleared his throat a couple times and then he said, 'I don't reckon you was figurin' to be ridin' my way, was you? I ain't so crazy about my own company as some folks. If you're goin' my way I'll hang fire an' ride with you. I got a feelin' here lately— Sometimes I wake with the sweat all over me thinkin' I've been throwed an' hung a foot in the stirrup.' He shuddered, 'That's a hard way to die.'

*　　　*　　　*

Them words of his wouldn't get out of my head. Over and over and over I kept hearing them like a kind of refrain to the sound of our hoofbeats. I tried to get my mind worked up about Lovelee, about that dadblasted kid and that Texican, Driver, but all I could think of was them damn words. They was a kind of an echo that kept bouncing back at me. I tried to see in my mind the face of Bluff's sister but all I could see was that foot in the stirrup, that

106

down-hanging leg and the shape bounding after it.

I got so worked up by them words I was sweating. I got to imagining all kind of things, like maybe the old gent *did* have a bolt loose; the way he'd been acting was sure queer enough. But I couldn't believe it. I kept seeing them dust-covered clothes of Jim Varlance and Jim's twisted foot in another gent's boot.

Had this old feller been trying to say something? Trying, maybe, to tell me something about Jim? 'That's a hard way to die'—I kept hearing him say it and then I would see his bony shoulders shudder.

I was thinking about it as we walked our horses away from the Springs. We set off without talk for the mouth of the draw. It wasn't much over a couple of hundred yards off. And all that way I kept turning it over. It looked pretty near certain he'd tried to give me a tip but hadn't dared say much on account of Del Widney. It never entered my mind he might of meant what he'd said and that his scare might of been pure and simple for himself.

He'd been scared, all right. He had been scared plenty. But I figured it was on account of Drumm might find out he'd been riding, with Strump which Drumm didn't like no better than poison. I figured Les was scared Cal Drumm might up and fire him.

I was still curious to know why he'd been up

107

there with Strump to a place as off-trail and
unused as Gisela. I even thought a little bit I
might take a run up there, but mostly I thought
about them last words of Trumbet's and
wondered if he'd get round to saying any
more.

But them words of Les Trumbet's and
Trumbet's queer actions wasn't all the odd
things I had on my mind. Just before we had
started away from Tailpiece, Widney had give
me a private kind of look and hooked one
shoulder toward the door of his shanty. When
I followed him in he had give me an earful and
it wasn't of the sort to rest a man's mind none.

'You wanta watch out for that feller,' he
said. 'That old coot has got a rope draggin',
mister. Did you know Harry Bluff put him
outa the cow business? Well, it's so an', by
grab, ol' Les ain't fergot it. The way he prowls
this country at night . . .'

He let the rest trail off and looked up at me
sly like. 'Damn handy guy with a knife, that
feller.'

You would think a guy which had been
fighting rustlers around that country would of
been a heap smarter than to go dashing round
with a hat full of notions. You'll probably grant
I had plenty to think about, but a man in a
saddle ain't got no business thinking. Any
feller with sense would of watched the
rimrocks.

It took a blue whistler to wake me up.

108

We'd got into the draw and was jogging along, just rounding the bend, when the bullet come whanging down out of the oak brush.

I seen old Les lurch. I heard the grunt that come out of him. I seen him fold over and pitch from the saddle.

I grabbed out my rifle and dug in the steel. Hellity larrup we went for that smoke puff with me scattering lead all through them bushes, but that dry-gulching devil got clean away.

CHAPTER TWELVE

I hunted all over that arroyo but all I could find was where he had squatted. I found the shell but it didn't help out none. Plenty of guys packed .45-90's.

A cut-and-run killer. The same skunk, probably, that had wiped out Bluff and Varlance. And I hadn't no more idea who he was right then than I'd had staring down at that knife in Harry Bluff's back.

John Hughes, I reckoned, would of had that devil strung up by now—strung up or a sight too dead to skin. What would Burt Mossman be thinking of me? A fine lot of help to the governor I was!

I sure felt dauncy heading back to the horses. I pretty near felt like I'd killed him myself as I stood looking down at that pore crumpled shape. There was nothing I could do for the old feller now—nothing, I mean, that would do him any good. That slug had took him square between the eyes.

I felt plumb sick. I couldn't look at him. The killer had meant that bullet for me and pore old Les had rid right into it.

Or had he?

Suddenly wondering, I put up a stick in the trail for a marker and clambered back up to the bushwhacker's hide-out. I set my boots in his tracks same as he had and got myself down and took a look through the chaparral.

I could see all right he hadn't fired at me. He'd been after old Les and had sure as hell got him.

It was plain enough now Les had plenty reason for the fright I had seen staring out of his face. Someway or another he had found out something which the killer hadn't cottoned to have passed around.

I still couldn't see how the guy had got onto it. Of course, naturally, I seen I didn't know much about Les. Drumm was paying him range boss wages and he hadn't looked worth them; he had explained that to me by calling it charity. Les had, I mean. Del Widney had told me Les prowled at night: I didn't know if I could believe Widney or not. I had seen Les with Strump at Gisela. When I'd started to mention it, Les's eyes had stopped me and my staring had called Widney's notice to it.

Mulling things over it seemed a plenty smart notion to go back down to Widney's and look around some. If Widney's horse had been ridden— If he was short on breath—

I got up from my squatting and was patting the brush when the floggeting sound of a fast-running horse whipped me halfway round and left me, froze like, staring. A horsebacker bulged round the bend in the trail and come fogging the dust right up to our horses. He pulled up in the dust with his bronc on its haunches and piled from the saddle and run toward where Les lay in the trail. I caught the flash of metal and jerked up my rifle. I was just getting fixed to squeeze the trigger when it come over me sudden the guy wasn't a him.

It was a she, by grab, and she was dressed like a man with her hair pushed tight up under her hat. I watched her stare at old Les—seen her back off, nervous. I seen the quick look she flung raking round her. She was jumping for her horse when I yelled through the bushes:

'Hold it!'

She stopped so short she nearly tipped herself over. No Injun could of froze stiller than she done.

'Mebbe you better throw down that gun.'

She didn't look round. The only thing she moved at all was her fingers when she let the gun fall.

'Stand right where you are,' I said. 'I'll be

down.'

* * *

It was Lovelee.

She give a nervous little laugh. Her cheeks was like wood ash.

'Thank God!' she cried, and come toward me, shaking. 'Oh, Dan—I'm so frightened!'

'You got good reason to be,' I growled and, like I'd struck her across the face, she stopped. Her lips come away from her teeth. Her eyes stared.

'You— Surely you can't believe I did that!'

I didn't say if I did or I didn't. I had been took in enough in this business and wasn't minded to get took in again. All the worry and battlement, all the worst that was in me, rose up and took hold of my nature then. I said without thinking, 'You better explain what you're doin' here, Lovelee. It's a pretty far piece from the Straddle Bug ranch house.'

I was bone-tired—dog-tired. I didn't know if I was coming or going or I wouldn't of took that tone with her. It wrenched me to see her look that way, to feel all the miles she shoved between us. But my dander was up. I wasn't backtracking. I hadn't been sent here to play squire to women, and the head that was turned by a pretty face could swift be the head of a mighty dead corpse.

'Quick!' I said. 'You goin' to answer or ain't

112

you?'

It looked for a minute like maybe she was. Then a wind went racketing through the brush and color chased some of the drowned look out of her, 'I came here,' she said, fetching up her chin, 'to get a—' She looked at me and said, 'to be alone.'

'You sure picked a place!' I told her, gruff. 'Alone with a dead man. That's a damn good alibi!'

She swayed against the shove of the wind. There was something I couldn't read back of her stare.

'Where was you at when you heard the shot?'

Her mouth kind of tightened. She was staring at me like she couldn't believe it. She said, breathing hard, 'I didn't think you could be like that, Dan. I thought you were bigger—I thought you were honest.'

'Honest!' I said, glaring back at her. 'You're a great one to start sayin' things about honest!'

I guess I was pretty near shouting. It wasn't her fault things had happened this way. She couldn't of been wanting it no more than I did; but I wasn't fit to be talked to right then. This business was murder, and here she was mixed right in the middle of it, getting in deeper every time she breathed.

'Look,' I said. 'First we find your old man. A gent he's had words with gets took off the same evening. He gets killed in a place your old man warned him out of. He was met by a woman that was waitin' there for him. He starts for the horse pen to put up his bronc. He don't get more than ten-foot away when a forty-five slug caves the back of his face in. By God, what would *you* think if *I* was that woman?'

There was just the two of us, nothing else counted. I forgot where we was. I forgot Trumbet's body. I forgot the cold wind blowing down off the mountain. I couldn't see nothing but the look of her eyes.

'I'd at least give the woman a chance to tell her side.'

'You're the woman,' I said. 'Start tellin' it then.'

She never opened her mouth.

'I don't claim you done it,' I told her. 'But you was there an' you better start scratchin' your head for a story. That inquest is likely to bring out some facts. Drumm found a handkerchief. It's all over blood an' it smells clean to Greenback. There won't be no doubt it belongs to you.'

All I could see was them eyes of hers staring.

'If your old man an' Sloan was sure enough friends—'

'Do you think I bake pies for my father's enemies?'

'I ain't thinkin',' I said, 'I'm tryin' to find out. What was your brother doin' up at Gisela

114

five weeks ago?'

'He went up there on business.'

'To Gisela?' I looked at her. 'I thought all you Bluffs done your business to Greenback.'

She flung up her head. She give me back glare for glare. 'The Bluffs do their business wherever it suits them!'

'Yeah! That pride—' I snarled, and caught myself. I said, 'This thing is murder, try to keep that in mind. Now when you met Jim Varlance at Sloan's last night—'

'I didn't meet Jim Varlance at Sloan's last night.'

'Your tracks is scattered all over that yard! Why lie? Lyin' won't get you outa this! Do you *wanta* be charged with killin' him? You want Drumm to tell how you went there an' met him? How the two of you stood in them trees an' argued? How you shot him quick as he turned his back? You want Drumm to tell how he was drug by a stirrup an' show that jury where you kneeled on the ground to jerk off his boots an' put on his feet the ones that was wore by your father's killer? Is *that* what you want?'

The look of her eyes tore the guts right out of me.

She run to her horse like a hunted badger. The wind caught the beat of its hoofs and lost them.

I was left, cold and sick, with my thoughts and Les Trumbet.

115

CHAPTER THIRTEEN

Drumm's crew was round the chuck wagon in a camp at the mouth of Skunktracks Canyon two miles south of the Brad and Dash when I found them on my way back from town. I had packed Les Trumbet in to the coroner. I had done a whole pile of round and round thinking and turned up some things I figured to work on. I had ought to of guessed who the killer was then, but it had not quite come over me yet. There was some things I wanted to ask a few people. I wanted to find out what kind of business had took the kid to that tumble-down town at about the same time Bluff had set off for Willcox. I wanted to know why they'd both quit their bunch again last night on that trip to Roblero's, and what Tom Driver was so wild-eyed hunting when he'd come busting into the cook shack this evening.

So far I'd been playing this hand with my eyes shut and I'd about all of that fun I wanted. If somebody's mouth didn't loosen right sudden I was in good case to loosen somebody's teeth up. I had done all the blundering round I aimed to.

According to the doc, if I could believe him, Jim Varlance had died between seven and seven-thirty. Then Bluff had been killed, between seven-thirty and eight. Varlance had

116

been found at his ranch around ten. Bluff had been found at the Straddle Bug about two hours later when his crew and kin had got home from Roblero's. And then, this evening. Les Trumbet had been killed. Drumm had been paying Les Trumbet wages. Was those wages being paid for Trumbet's after-dark prowling? What had Trumbet been doing with Strump at Gisela?

It still seemed to me like them killings hadn't nothing to do with no range feud, but I had a strong hunch this could easy become one if something didn't bust my way in a hurry. This country was set on too hair-edged a temper to let them killings go long unregarded. Both them outfits wanted Sloan's basin. Rafter had grabbed it. I had talked Drumm into moving out but it was a cinch he'd string with me only just so far. If he thought for a minute Driver'd throw *his* stuff in there, or if Driver *did*—

It was then I wondered where the hell Driver's crew was.

I pulled up my horse and set there scowling. It was too damned likely they was gathering their cattle.

I come near lamming for the Straddle Bug then. The only thing that stopped me was my nearness to Drumm's camp. I had to see Drumm. I had to check on Les Trumbet, and a couple extra miles, I figured, wouldn't make no difference.

Maybe, I thought, I had ought to warn Drumm. But my next thought told me I had better not. If Rafter and Straddle Bug ever come together over a thing like who was to browse Sloan's basin, this place was a whole heap likely to look like beef day at a Injun agency.

I jogged on again toward where I could see the dust of Drumm's cattle. And the more I thought the more it seemed like the smart thing to do was to keep my mouth shut. So far, anyway, as the Straddle Bug crew went. I would see what Drumm had to say about Trumbet, see what new cause he had dug up for trouble, and then cut west for Bluff's place on the Tonto. There was no use getting my bowels in a uproar. I would look pretty foolish if Driver's crew was to home.

I rolled up a smoke but it hadn't no flavor. I pitched it away and rode up to Drumm's wagon.

His men was eating. They kept on eating. I could see where they'd bedded the herd off yonder. They had three-four fellers riding circle. They was all packing rifles like they looked for trouble.

Drumm waved a hand. He told me cordial, 'Help yourself. Grab a plate an' pitch in.'

I tried not to see that sow bosom pie or sniff at the appetizing smells that was curling up out of them pots hanging over the coals. I shook my head regretful like and hoped he would

118

savvy what a martyr I was.

'I'll be takin' mine Spanish for tonight, I reckon.' Taking it Spanish was what folks said when they tightened up their belts as a substitute for chuck. 'Time's a-burnin' an' I got to be ridin'. Any chance of me gettin' a fresh horse from you?'

'When the Law needs a horse it don't need to ask the Rafter.' He waved a hand at the remuda. 'Cut out what you want.'

I rode over and done it. I cut me out a zebra dun and a powerful looking bald-faced bay, just in case I happened to need a spare. Then I changed my mind and let the dun go. I throwed my hull on the bay and rode back. I give Drumm the eye and he got up without talk and followed me off to the north of the wagon.

'How many cattle's Strump got in this bunch?'

'Couple of hundred.'

'How well do you know him?'

'About as well as I want to.'

'Any new light on what happened to Varlance?'

'We found the grub.'

When it got plain he wasn't going to enlarge none I said, 'Where?'

'Under them cottonwoods, buried in the weeds.'

It looked like Varlance had been killed on Sloan's place all right. 'But that still don't prove it was the girl,' I said. 'You could of done it yourself. There's some that allows you has mighty good reason—'

'Strump an' the Straddle Bugs. They would,' Drumm said. 'Is that what *you* think?'

'I ain't got around to the thinkin' stage yet.'

Drumm showed me a skeptical grim. He said, 'I hope you're keepin' a eye on Driver.'

'What do you mean by that?'

'Well, you've got us out of Sloan's basin now. I would hate to see Tom Driver move in there.'

His eyes said a whole heap more than that.

'You can leave that part to me,' I said. 'He won't move in there without the kid says to.'

'I wouldn't bank too heavy on that. Driver might have a axe of his own to grind. Way I read his sign he ain't the kind to take orders from no kid. He didn't get on too well with Bluff, an' now Bluff's gone—' He spread out his hands in a disclaiming gesture. 'You better watch that feller. Ain't you recognized him yet?'

He grinned at my look.

'His tail gets over the lines mighty easy. Didn't you know he used to be with the Rangers? Company D—Captain John Hughes' outfit.'

'Driver?'

'Driver.' Drumm nodded. 'Surprises you, does it?' I reckon he's been a surprise to a lot of folks. I don't know much about the insides of it but I think he got to kicking over the traces. I've a notion he was a little too quick on the trigger to suit friend Johnny. He got out of them parts between dark an' dawn.'

'An' how do you know all that?'

Drumm grinned that thin tight grin of his. 'You could check with Hughes. If you had more time.'

'Yeah,' I said. 'If I had more time I could do a lot of things.'

But it was a new angle. No getting around that. I'd been thinking of Driver all the time as Bluff's foreman. A number of things come into my mind then. Driver's tough ways. Driver's looks at young Bluff and the kid's looks at Driver. That division of authority I had sensed last night.

'What kind of axe would he have to grind?'

Drumm shrugged. His glance went off toward the herd and come back again.

'If this is another of your sign-readin' acts—' I said.

'You better play this smart an' keep your eye on him if you don't want folks to set their guns goin'.'

I considered him a while in a kind of silence. It struck me he knowed a lot more than he was saying.

I said, 'You got any more stuff hid up your sleeve? Mebbe you could tell me when Hack Sloan disappeared.'

'I can sure do that. It was about five weeks

121

ago. I dropped by his place one afternoon. He was just saddlin' up for a trip to Gisela. He—'

'To Gisela!'

'Sure.' Drumm looked at me. 'He was goin' up after some grub, he said. If you'd seen him that day you'd of thought he was needin' some. I never seen that old man so pore. Claimed he'd been on short rations for a couple of weeks. Hadn't dared leave the place for fear Bluff would jump him.'

'Jump *him*,' I said, 'or his place?'

'The place, I guess. He didn't look scared on his own part. He was sure in a lather about that place, though. Told me Bluff's men was ridin' all through the rimrocks, jest waitin' for a chance to ketch him gone an' take over. I told him they was probably watchin' for cow thieves but he begged me to stay there until he got back. You see, he was homesteadin' that part up around his buildings, an'—'

'Then, if anythin' happened to him—'

Drumm's glance was plenty meaningful. 'That's about the size of it. Only, so far, Bluff ain't made no effort to move in.'

Playing it cautious to keep clear of the government. I said, 'Did you stay.'

'I hung around until four the next evenin'.'

'And he hadn't got back in that time?'

'He hadn't come back when I left,' Drumm said.

It didn't look good. It didn't look good at all.

'Wasn't you suspicious" I asked.

'I didn't like it.' Drumm said, 'But after all, you know, somethin' might of come up to change his plans. He might of gone north to try an' find him some help. He hadn't been able to keep on no local boys. Things happened to 'em. Misfortunate things that give the place a bad name.'

'So you went home an' talked it over with Varlance, I reckon, an' the two of you decided to move Rafter in, eh?'

'No,' Drumm said, 'not right off we didn't. We decided to wait a while an' see what happened. But when a month went by and he still hadn't showed we made up our minds somethin' must of happened to him. We rode over one day an' took a good look around. There was a dried-up pie settin' shriveled on the table an' a couple dead rats layin' shriveled beside it. We seen a lot of Bluff's cattle feedin' off Sloan grass. That was when we made up our minds. We shoved Bluff's stuff out an' come after our own.'

I thought about that. I thought of some other things. I wondered whose boots we had found on Jim Varlance. I wondered how far Hack Sloan had got and if he'd been killed or if, scared like he was, he'd yanked loose of his rope and quit the country. He could of done that. Plenty of other guys had. I wondered what had happened to the bloody clothes the killer had worn when he'd packed Bluff around.

There was a pile to do.

'You an' Sloan ever have any run-ins?' I said.

'Would Sloan be askin' me to watch his place—'

'I don't know that he did. I only got your word for it.'

'Well, that's right.' Drumm grinned. 'You don't have to believe it.'

'Ever get tough with him? Shove him around?'

Drumm's eyes bored into me. 'I don't go around beatin' up old men. I'm in the cow business, friend. It takes all my time tryin' to make me a livin'.'

'Did you think it would help to have Trumbet for ramrod?'

'So you heard about that?'

'A kinda curious choice.'

'Nothin' curious about it.' Drumm's tone was gruff. 'I come up pretty wild, never had no raisin'. Never had nobody to give a damn till I'd learned all the orneriness no kid ought to know. I got my schoolin' in the cow camps, Waggoner, doin' the things growed men was too good for.'

He considered me darkly.

'I ain't whinin', savvy? I'm tryin' to tell you about Les Trumbet. He was a owner then. His Panther Springs ranch was a goin' concern, an' a hell-tearin' good one. He heard about me.

124

Never had no one of his own to look out for, hadn't never got married. He come over to Payson one day an' fetched me.'

He stood a while, quiet, like he was thinking back to it. 'Les give me a job at a growed hand's pay an' he took the trouble to see that I earned it. What I know about ranchin' I learned from him. A man can't talk about them things, Waggoner.'

'Bluff froze him out, eh?'

'Matter of fact, he bought him out. Give him about ten cents on the dollar.'

I could see he had said about all he aimed to. The look of his eyes was cold and glintin'.

'Where was Les the day you stayed over at Sloan's?'

Drumm looked at me careful. 'Mebbe you better ask him.'

'I'm askin' you.'

'I don't know,' Drumm said. 'But I can tell you this. He wasn't off killin' Hack Sloan, if that's botherin' you.'

'He might of been up round Gisela though.'

We looked at each other. 'You think mebbe he seen somethin'?' Drumm said.

'I don't know what I'm thinkin',' I said. 'This is the orneriest mess I ever mixed into.'

Maybe I ought to of told him then. If a guy knowed when and what he ought to do I reckon this world would be a heap different place.

But I didn't tell Drumm that Les Trumbet

125

was dead. The facts of the matter was I plain didn't dare to. Not after what he had just told me about him. I was scairt he would go and dig up the hatchet. I was scairt he would head plumb straight for the Straddle Bug. I wasn't hunting for *more* trouble; I was up there to stop what they already had.

I decided to put a few questions that was bothering me.

'How much do you know about young Bluff's habits? Do you know if he ever rides out of this country? If he ever goes off on a visit to friends?'

'If he's got any friends,' Drumm said, 'I ain't heard of 'em. Don't chew, don't drink, never plays no cards.' He curled his lip. 'A reg'lar pillar of virtue. Thinks the Bluffs is too good for the rest of us rabble. All that kid ever thinks of is horses.'

'He went up to Gisela not so long ago.'

'I heard about that. Horses again. Hung around there two days tryin' to buy him some race stock, but the guy never showed.'

'What do you know about Strump? Has he got a sick mother?'

'They say she gets down with the shakin' fever. I ain't never seen her.'

'How'd he come to run cattle with you?'

'He made a deal with Jim. I hadn't nothin' to do with it. That was always Jim's trouble,' Drumm growled, disgusted. 'Couldn't never turn nobody down.'

'He was over to the Bluffs.' Seemed on pretty good terms with them for a feller that's been runnin' his cattle with you.'

'Jude plays the percentages,' Drumm said dryly. 'Bein' on good terms with folks pays him dividends. It's a wonder his pants ain't got postholes in 'em.'

'Plays politics, eh?'

'It's a business with him. He's got a ranch in the Gallups, near the Pleasant Valley trail. About the same kind of browse as the rest of us depends on, nothin' very excitin', but good enough most times. This has been a bad year. We been short on water. We've all got more critters than we've got any feed for—expect you've noticed that. It's the reason we've all been watchin' Sloan's basin. There's good grass in there, a heap more than Hack's usin'.'

He fetched out his plug and bit off some tobacco.

'The Bluffs is the only ones that ain't faced with feedin'. They've got a lot more range than the rest of us fellers. A lot more, an' better. Gettin' range has been Harry Bluff's main passion ever sinst I've knowed him. He's got a big hunk of range. He's got it pretty well stocked.'

'I thought I heard he'd been buyin' more cattle?'

Drumm give me another of them tight grins. I seen what he wanted to make me think. He wanted me to think Bluff was buying them cattle to put in the basin and eat up Sloan's grass. Well, maybe he had been, but I reckoned long before them cattle was delivered this fight for Rattlesnake would be past history. It was past history now if I had anything to say about it.

It was time I was having me a talk with Tom Driver. I took my leg down off of the horn.

Drumm said, 'Strump went to Sloan with the idea of leasin' but Hack turned him down. Strump made a play to stand in with the Bluffs then. It was about this time that Sloan turned up missin'. Then Strump sees the Rafter gettin' ready to move in so he comes yowlin' round talkin' old friends an' neighbors.' He said, 'I sometimes think Jim was soft in the head.'

'Strump won't be a heap pleased when he hears you've moved out of there.'

'Likely not.'

'He may ask you to cut his stuff out.'

'He may ask it.'

In a roundabout way I kind of had to admire Drumm. Most of the time he was calm as a horse trough. No paw and no beller. But I felt pretty certain he would do what he said.

He hitched up his belt and spit out his tobacco.

I don't know why it was but I begun to feel cold down my belt buckle, and the way of the wind hadn't nothing to do with it.

'I've found out,' he said, 'whose boots Jim

Varlance was wearin'.'

I knowed it was coming. He was being too quiet.

'Lovelee's!' I blurted.

'No, her brother's—young Dandy's.'

CHAPTER FOURTEEN

There was snow in the wind when I set out. I didn't really want to go to Gisela; I was being drawn there against all of my wishes. My wishes, right then, was to hit out for the Straddle Bug by the shortest route. I wanted to see Lovelee. I wanted to talk to that kid. There was a number of things I wanted to say to Tom Driver, things that was needing to be said in a hurry if half what I'd heard from Drumm was the truth. I should get hold of Roblero. I ought to go and see Strump. But I was only one guy and one guy can't be everywhere. Time was a-burning and that inquest was set for high noon tomorrow. So I made what I figured was the smartest choice. I got directions from Drumm and set out for Gisela.

There was nothing a man could like in the prospect. A long tough ride, uphill for the most part, over travel I knew precious little about. It's true I'd come into this country by way of Gisela, but I'd come down the west side of Tonto Creek. I was east of it now, a long ways east, and it was getting dark fast. I might get lost. I might run into a blizzard and get snowed in. It never crossed my mind I might run into the killer and catch me a dose of what caught Trumbet. I was too stirred up right then about Lovelee. I could see what a jury might do with them boots. And if Drumm got up and done his sign-reading act there wasn't no doubt in my head what would happen.

Night fell swift as I bucked the steep benches to the north of Sloan's basin. I was tired as a dog and had more troubles than a rat-tailed horse tied short in fly time. On top of everything else there was the fear in my mind this might be a wild goose chase. It was after I'd slicked my saddle about a hour that it run through my mind I ought to stop by Jude Strump's.

I really owed it to myself to check Lovelee's story. I told myself it was my duty to do it, but I argued quite a spell before I got myself round to it. Even then I didn't want to. I said it was because I couldn't waste the time; and I couldn't, that was certain, but it wasn't the reason. Suppose Strump's mother said she hadn't been up there?

She had told me herself, just that afternoon, that she hadn't seen Varlance at Sloan's the night before, but when I thought that over I seen it didn't mean much. She hadn't said she hadn't met Varlance, and she hadn't said she hadn't been at Sloan's. All she had claimed was that she hadn't met Varlance there; and if Strump's mother told me Lovelee hadn't been to *her* house . . .

I give it up and with a growl I swung the bay further north. I had a damn guilty feeling about wasting that time. I was sure in advance it was going to be wasted. Even if Mrs. Strump told me Lovelee had been there that wouldn't he much comfort if, while I was learning it, somebody else got killed. And it was quite in the cards somebody else might get killed. They would damn sure get killed if Driver shoved Bluff's cattle into Sloan's basin.

Them was no kind of thoughts to lug off through a snowstorm.

It wasn't storming yet but I could see it would be soon. The wind was rising, throwing its moaning wails through the timber. It was a hell of a night to be out in strange country. It was a hell of a night any way you looked at it.

We kept climbing steady. I wasn't pushing the bay but I was keeping him at it. It was no fun bracing that kind of a wind on the kind of a trail that run up through these rimrocks. In a way I was glad I couldn't see much. In this kind of country I could tell from experience that some of them drops would land you in China. I kept hugging the wall just as close as I could. I wasn't trying to steer the bay, I knowed enough not to. I said a few prayers for the quality of his feet and pulled my collar up

131

around my ears. I snagged the reins around the horn and shoved numbed fingers into my pockets. I had gloves on but a cowpuncher's gloves ain't much good for that weather.

It begun to snow in good earnest. I could see it settling on the mane of my horse, on the front of my coat and on the legs of my pants. It wasn't powdery stuff. It was big wet flakes that come down like a curtain. It was beginning to stick in the trail and in the scraggly brush that sometimes growed from the wall. I was seldam glad when we come out on a level and left the cliffs behind.

I tried to get my mind off the snow by thinking. I tried to get my mind off thinking by watching the snow. Thinking made me miserable; the snow did, too. It kept getting down the inside of my collar. I wished I'd never heard of Burt Mossman.

Then I got to fretting about Driver. Instead of coming up here I should of gone out and braced him. I should of made him tell me where that crew of his was or, failing that, I should of gone out and found them.

Like the straw that busted the camel's back, it's the little things, mostly, that frets a man, chafing and rubbing till his mind's plumb raw, and that is the way it was with me. The little things growed out of all proportion. I expect the weather had a heap to do with my dauncy outlook, but I had boggled this play from soda to hock and it growed on me with a kind of dread that I was backing another busted flush.

I was half in the notion of turning back. I might of done it, too, if I'd knowed where I was. But I hadn't no more idea than my saddle. With the snow coming down like the way it was, and all that twisting and turning I'd done, I couldn't tell back from forward hardly.

I don't know how come but we was going downhill.

I could tell by the feeling, not from what I could see. I couldn't see nothing but them damn falling snowflakes; I couldn't rightly even see them, just a snow-blurred darkness without any substance. But we was off the trail, I know that much. No horse is going to flounder around like mine was doing with packed ground under him. He hadn't no trail and the both of us knowed it. It took all the strength and balance I had to stay in that saddle the way we was weaving. I damn near choked the apple off.

Lucky for me the wind wasn't hitting me. But it still was blowing—up above and below me. Up above I didn't mind, but the thought of it blowing below scared me. Its booming echoes come rolling up like beat out of a drum with a boot heel. I forgot in that moment all I knowed about horses. I sawed on the reins like a greener. I was yanking the bay's head around when it happened. I heard the screech of his shoes go clanging off rock. I felt bunched muscles strain and jerk. He was going as I

133

flung myself from the saddle going out from under me into the black bitter howl of the wind.

I struck creviced rock and clung to it, shaking, with my face in the snow and my ears wildly ringing to that one last terrible cry from the bay.

*   *   *

There's no way of telling how long I laid there. I didn't do nothing. I didn't think even. I was most nigh scairt to draw my breath out of fear it might be the last I did draw. The lip of that chasm might be right at my back. It might be in front of me, beyond my head, or below my feet. I didn't know which way the lip of that thing was and the slightest move might send me over it. The rock might come away in my hand.

Time hadn't no meaning. But it finally commenced to sift through my head that my hands couldn't hold to that rock forever. Already they was cramping bad. They was getting numb with the cold besides. I knowed they was bound to bust loose mighty soon and if I didn't crave to join my horse it was high time I was doing something about it.

Mighty careful I begun feeling round with my foot. Nothing happened. I tried to move the other foot. Pins and needles run up to my leg and I thought for a second I must of broke it, but a break would of felt a heap worse than that. I breathed again. It was numb, of course, from stopped circulation on account of it being wedged hard against rock. I'd been laying on it also and the damn thing had been half froze to start with.

I hadn't the guts to reach down and rub it. To reach down I'd of had to let go my hold. I didn't know what to do hardly. And besides all that I was getting plumb chilled.

I begun to shake. I begun to feel desperate. If I didn't get up out of this pretty quick I might not be *able* to get up out of it. I might as well fall in the canyon as to lay there and freeze to death.

When that thought come over me I shook some more. My jaws was clamped so tight my teeth ached but I made myself unloose one hand. Not a thing happened. I felt kind of foolish. I unpried the grip of my other cramped fist and still nothing happened.

I took a deep breath. Cold sweat run down my neck like water. There was snow-slippery rock underneath my right hand; there was more slippery rock all around, it seemed like. I eased over on my belly and lay a while, panting.

Pretty soon I begun to feel better. I twisted myself around and set up. I slapped my gloved hands to get some life back in them and rubbed some feeling into my legs. My ears was colder than snakes with the hide off. I put snow on them and started kicking my feet. I couldn't stay there all night, that was certain.

They say lost people always move in circles. I sure didn't want to do that. I had to move or hunt shelter. I had to move to do it.

It was still snowing hard.

I drew up my knees and put down my left hand to get my feet under me. Luckily I didn't put no weight on it. There wasn't nothing under it to put no weight on. There wasn't nothing under it but the canyon.

CHAPTER FIFTEEN

I got the shakes so bad again it didn't look like I would ever get shed of them. When I finally catched ahold of the jerk-line. I was wallering along through the drifts and shallers like a bull-whacker looking down the neck of a bottle.

I seen it was time I got onto myself.

I hadn't no idea how long I'd been walking nor where that walking had fetched me to, but the scenery looked to of changed considerable. I was in what seemed to be rolling country and the night wasn't near as dark as it had been. There was quite a passle of second-growth pine shoving up through the flakes that was still coming down.

There was teeth in the wind and it was

getting colder. I ain't never been no hand for much walking, but walking right then looked better than dying. You couldn't stand still in that kind of weather without you wanted to freeze up solid. I had to find some way to get out of that wind.

I put it behind me. It made walking easier if there was such a thing as any ease to it. I wondered what quarter the wind was coming out of. If it was coming from the north like it had been when I started, facing into it, I thought, would be taking me in the direction of Gisela, the place I had set out for. But it might of changed. I might of come too far right or left of the trail to get through by following any such notion.

About that time something juned up a working at the back of my mind I was not alone. I took a good look round over my shoulder. I couldn't see nothing more than twenty foot off. I couldn't see nothing inside of that distance but that everlasting snow and the dim blurred shapes of half a dozen pines. I couldn't hear nothing but the wind rushing through them, but my unease growed.

I begun to think I was followed. I bent my head and started bucking the wind.

I reckoned I was going uphill again, up a kind of a ridge or hogback. The pines fell away out of reach of my eyes. The snow closed in like a dirty gray curtain and there just didn't seem to be no end to it. I stumbled into a

137

floundering run and the next thing I knowed I was flat in the snow. I listened to the wind howling past above me and for the first time that night I begun to feel warm.

People usually feels warmer when they're starting to freeze.

I clawed up out of it. A darkness begun to press in round me and I begun beating on myself with my hands and stamping my feet till my half-froze limbs cried out for mercy. But I wouldn't let them have it. I wouldn't give in. I kept beating myself till I hurt all over. Burt Mossman hadn't sent me here to die. He had sent me up here to do a job of work and no storm was going to stop me.

The collar of my coat was a icy ring against the backs of my ears and the sides of my cheekbones. I swore when I thought of the Hashknife bunkhouse and the boys playing cards around the pot-bellied stove. I cursed everything I could put my tongue to but I kept on going.

I don't know why, but I thought of the knife I had pulled out of Bluff, and I thought of Les Trumbet's talk about it, and suddenly the wind seemed a mighty lot colder.

It was getting lighter again. I come into a place where the cold didn't bite so. I could see trees huddled along the side of a cleared space. I seemed to be down in some kind of a pocket and the feeling of being followed got stronger. It didn't make sense and I knowed it didn't but the feeling stayed with me. I got to stopping and listening but all I could hear was the wind whistling through the shaggy stems of the pinetops.

And then the wind suddenly quit.

For a second I'd of swore I heard horse hoofs behind me. I whirled like a cornered wolf with bared teeth, but all I could see was that fluttering whiteness, all I could hear was the hush of its silence. The air was like breath coming out of a icebox but I wasn't concerned with the cold no more. I was wondering when that lost knife would find me.

*   *   *

I seen the black smudge of timber ahead. I gritted my teeth and went floundering toward it. I meant to get in its shelter. I meant to wait there and see what camped on my back trail.

Not that I was in much doubt about it. I reckoned it was the killer, determined to be rid of me for once and for all. He couldn't of picked a better time nor place. In the drifting snow of these high mountain meadows I might lay hid till spring. I might never be found.

I reached the pines. I went plowing into the down—swinging branches filling my ears and collar with snow. I took off my coat with a mutter and shook it. I put it back on and pulled off my gloves that was crackly with ice and scrubbed both hands with snow to warm them. I thrust them, gloveless, deep into my pockets and, after a while, I took to rubbing them. I blowed on the right one, done all I could think that might help to shape it to the need of my pistol. And I wondered again what the killer had done with the bloody clothes and Jim Varlance's boots.

It's funny the stuff that will prowl through your head when you ain't looking round for no thoughts at all. Fragments, queer notions, all kind of wild fancies; like why had Jude Strump gone this noon to the Straddle Bug, and what had roused such black hate in Tom Driver.

I stared through the down-drifting gloom and saw nothing. Nerves and this storm and no sleep was what ailed me. I said so again with a worn kind of fury. No man could track another through this, nor no woman could. Only a feller raised up in these mountains and knowing the place I had recent set out for could hope to come up with me now, and nobody knowed where I had set out for but—

Them was the kind of thoughts loony ticks had. It wouldn't never hold water; it must break plumb apart in the light of cold reason. No two guys could— Why, the old man would of— But hadn't Drumm claimed Bluff had gone off to Willcox to fetch in more cattle? And what could Hack Sloan ever of had to do with it? And why should old Trumbet—

But it fit! I could pretty nigh hear the pieces locking down into place. I must get to Gisela, I must talk to that barkeep! Gisela was where old Hack Sloan had been bound for. Gisela was where I'd seen Strump with Les Trumbet—Gisela tied everything all in together. It tied in young Dandy who'd gone up to buy horses, it tied in the boots for the guy couldn't wear them and it tied in Tom Driver, the ex-Texas Ranger, and that black glowering hate that looked out of his eyes.

It explained why the kid had gone off on his horse and what Driver'd been hunting when he come barging into the cook shack so wild like. Standing under them branches I thought of old Trumbet, of his dreary frustrations, his scared eyes and his night-riding; and I thought of the things Del Widney had told me, of Drumm's gruff remarks and the little I knowed of the man's own actions; and I felt the hair start to prickle at the back of my scalp.

The shape of a rider come floundering toward me.

He was going on past when I stepped out, gun ready.

'Right here,' I said, and Moran yelled 'Hey!'

'What's the big idea chousin' after me that way?'

'Keep your thanks fer Drumm—he's the fefler that reckoned you was goin' t' git lost.'

'How'd you know where to find me?'

'Hell, I didn't—I was goin' by!'

'You come mighty close.'

'Well, we figgered about where you'd git off

141

the trail. I struck out right for it. Thought I seen you a couple of times but I couldn't make sure.'

I said, 'It looks mighty odd, him sendin' you after me.'

'He sure wa'n't hankerin' t' hev you die in no blizzard.'

'Is he watchin' them cattle? Is he watchin' the passes?'

'Like a hawk,' Moran grinned.

'All right,' I said. 'I've lost my horse. Give me a hand up an' we'll lam for Gisela. I want a trail to that town that'll take us past Strump's.'

'You think Strump done it?' Moran exclaimed.

'Time's a-burnin',' I said.

*   *   *

We rode into the yard of Strump's Boxed K to find the place darker than hell with the fire out. 'Gone t' bed,' Moran grunted, but that wasn't the way I sized it up. Cold fingers was feeling my backbone again. We climbed down off our horse in front of the porch. I knocked on the door with my snow-covered glove.

Nobody answered. No lights showed. The place looked deserted as Bluff's had looked the night before, but, remembering Bluff's, I was inclined to be careful. Moran fetched his gun up and hammered with that. Then be reached for the latch.

'Take it easy,' I said. 'I been told his mother has been pretty sick lately.'

'Must be mighty sick,' Moran said, 'not to hear that.' He kicked open the door and stood back with his gun out. When still nothing happened he sent a loud yell yammering around through the rooms. 'Hell,' he growled, 'this place is emptier'n a pan full of bubbles. Watch the door,' he said, whipping a match up his pants, and went clanking his spurs through the place like he owned it.

It didn't take long. There was only three rooms. Strump wasn't in them nor Strump's sick mother.

'Mebbe,' I said, 'he's took her in to the Doc.'

But I didn't believe it. Moran didn't, neither. I felt of the stove. I put a hand in the ashes and found them pretty near cold. I shook my head and he followed me out.

'Take the bunkhouse,' I said. 'I'll look through the barn.'

Strump's barn wasn't new but it was well built and roomy. There was eight box stalls and, across the other side, a long row of feed bins with harness hung over them from wooden pegs screwed into the wall boards. The whole top floor was piled deep with hay; I didn't go up but I could see that much without touching the ladder. The loft didn't go all the way across. It was two lofts, really, with a twelve-foot opening through the center of the

143

barn. Hay smell and horse smell was comforting odors. There was a couple nice saddles on their backs by the door and, off to one side, sacked feeds and fertilizer was piled ten deep.

It was a restful place in the light of the lantern I had found and lit. There was a stud munching hay at the last stall's manger. He looked up at the shine of the light and nickered. I went over past his stall and said howdy to him. I noticed his fetlocks was still pretty wet. He had been rubbed down but his coat was still steaming. I had seen this horse at the Straddle Bug; he had a face that a man would remember.

Idly staring around I found myself by the bins. I had a horseman's wonder what Strump was feeding and bent over the nearest and scooped up a handful. It was oats mixed with corn and a little rolled barley. I thought, if Lovelee has been here I had better make sure of it.

But how could I do that? There wasn't nobody home. I said, 'Anybody up in that loft?' and felt foolish. I hadn't looked for no answer and I sure didn't get one. I climbed up the ladder. I didn't see no one up there.

I come down and lounged by the feed bins again. I put a hand in the grain. I thought it looked kind of odd there wasn't nobody home, not even the woman who was supposed to be sick, a woman said to be down last week with the fever. It brought to mind Hack Sloan who had disappeared also, who had took a trip and never come back.

I stared at the grain, watched a couple of handfuls slide through my fingers while I asked myself where Strump's mother was.

I didn't pull down no answer, but my hand come onto something in that bin that stiffened me like I had grabbed up a rattler. It was cloth, by grab—a whole big wad of it. When I dug it out it was a shirt and some jeans. They was splattered with something that was stiff and dark.

My hands started shaking. I give a yell for Moran and kept on digging.

Moran come in grumbling and stamping off snow. 'There ain't nobody—'

His eyes stood out like a couple of saucepans. I knew what was coming before he said it.

'Them boots!' he stammered. 'Them's Jim Varlance's boots!'

CHAPTER SIXTEEN

We caught up a couple of last year's broncs from what had been left of Jude Strump's remuda, and lined out for Gisela. We left conversation to a time more convenient, but Moran had his thoughts and I had mine.

They was Jim's boots, I was satisfied, and the pants and shirt was the clothes the killer had worn last night while packing Bluff's body back home to the Straddle Bug.

Bluff, I figured, had been killed at Sloan's ranch. The killer, I reckoned, had been waiting there for him when Varlance come riding back from Del Widney's. I agreed with Drumm that they had probably talked some; I thought they had probably talked about Lovelee. I'd gone over that part so much in my mind I reckoned I could just about catch every movement; sometimes I almost could hear what was said.

In my own mind, I mean.

Either the killer or Varlance, I thought, had laid down the law in words that didn't need no explaining. My bets was on Varlance who had then turned away to put up his horse. The killer had come to Sloan's ranch to kill Bluff. Up till then, I thought, Jim Varlance hadn't entered the killer's plans at all. But the killer knowed Bluff was due to show any moment. He had to be rid of Jim Varlance pronto. Jim Varlance had died because he'd had the bad luck to ride into a trap that was set for murder.

The killer had done some mighty fast thinking. The shot that dropped Varlance fetched Bluff in a hurry. Varlance, falling, had hung a boot in the stirrup, Bluff, not Lovelee, busting into the yard, had seen Jim's shape being dragged by that horse and had took out after him. Bluff had got the horse stopped.

146

The killer, hid in the cottonwoods, had waited till Bluff was bent over Jim Varlance, then had sprung at him quickly and buried a skinning knife deep in Bluff's back.

Only then had the killer seen the fine chance offered to make these deaths seem like something they wasn't. The Rafter outfit, already distrusting the Straddle Bug, finding their boss sprawled dead in that yard, would he a heap likely to grab out their smoke poles without much thinking. Bluff, found stabbed in the back at the Straddle Bug, would work the same way on his crew. Each outfit, it looked like, would blame the other. With a pair of wrong-sized boots slicker-wrapped behind the cantle, the killer packed Bluff home. The killer took Dandy's boots and left a track by Bluff's body, and then, too clever by half, went back to Sloan's ranch and put the boots on Jim Varlance.

*   *   *

When we got to Gisela, there wasn't no lights in the town. The storm had quit, howled off to the south, and the stars was bright and cold above us as we stopped and swung down by the saloonkeeper's tie rack.

There was tracks in the snow drifted onto the porch.

Moran said, 'I doubt he's poundin' his ear very hard,' and banged on the door with the snout of his six-gun.

He must of been right. In almost no time at all we heard bedsprings creak. Bare feet hit the floor and come slapping toward us.

'Who—who is it?' a quavery voice called out nervous.

'Never mind who it is,' Moran growled impatient. 'Git that ~~god~~dam door open!'

We could hear old Whiskers fumble with the bar, then the door screaked open spilling lamplight out across the snow-covered planking. He was pulling up his pants as he backed away. He was somewhat disadvantaged by the lamp in his hand and peered at us worried like. 'I ain't got no—' He must of recognized me. He shut his face with a snap.

I said, 'When was the last time you seen Jude Strump?'

'Wh—what's—'

'You just answer the questions, I'll do the askin'. When was the last time you seen Strump around here?'

'You ort t' know—you was here,' Whiskers grumbled.

Moran said, suspicious, 'He ain't been here t'night?'

Whiskers said with a snarl, 'Would I lie t' you fellers?'

'We better not catch you,' I told him, crusty. 'Now, about five weeks ago Bluff was up here—'

'I guess you're meanin' young Dandy,

148

ain'tcha? *He* was up here about five weeks ago. Come up here t' meet some horse breedin' feller.'

'That's the time,' I said. 'Was Strump up here then?'

Whiskers shook his head. Curiosity was sure gnawing at that feller.

'Was Sloan or Les Trumbet?'

'Les Trumbet were here.'

'Did he talk to the kid? Did he seem worked up any?'

'Worked up how?' Whiskers said.

'Excited, I mean. Was he nervous, edgy?'

That old feller's eyes looked out at me funny. 'Seemed t' me about like he allus does, kinda down in the mouth. He dropped by fer some smokin'. Kid wasn't here, he was off with his horse—except he found things pretty dull around this place. First time he'd been here in three-four years. Does most of his tradin' to Greenback, I reckon.'

'How's Strump's mother been makin' out? Heard she was down with the fever,' I said.

'She was last week. I guess she'll prob'ly git over it. She allus has.'

'You sure Hack Sloan never come up here that time? Scratch your head for a little. Drumm says Hack told him he was comin' up here.'

'I can't help what Drumm says. I ain't seen Hack Sloan in over three months.'

I thought about that. I said, 'Aside from last

night, when was the last time you seen Jude Strump?'

He looked to be tired of the way I jumped round on him. He looked for a minute like he was considering telling me to go hop a horse for the hot place. Moran said dark like, 'This guy's a Ranger. You better talk up 'f you want to keep livin' healthy.'

Whiskers said, still scowling, 'He was around here pretty much all day yesterday.'

'He was!' Moran said. 'What the hell was he doin' up at this dead place?'

'Well, bein' you're askin', I don't mind sayin' I weren't took into his conference.'

'If you seen him,' I said—

'Yeah, I know. Save yer wind. He was pokin' around in them empty buildin's.'

Moran's jaw dropped. 'In them dillapity shacks?'

Whiskers scowled. 'I said so, didn't I?'

Moran looked busting to get right over there. I give him a warning eye and said, 'Who else was sashayin' round these parts while the kid was up here meetin' that horse breeder?'

The old man combed a hand through his mane and wriggled his lip to give a deep show of thinking. 'I sure can't call t' mind one soul. Ain't many folks comes by no more. Too out of the way. Nothin' here for 'em to come for now that Catawamp Annie's gone. We was glad t' hev the kid drop by. Now supposin' you tell me—'

150

'Who was this horse feller?' Moran cut in.

'Couldn't say,' Whiskers answered. 'He never showed up. The kid waited round here a couple of days before he finally give him up an' went on home. Some breeder from Texas, I think he said. S'posed t' hev some fast colts by a hoss called Eureka out of the McQuirter mare. Kid was all hopped up about 'em. Driver'd put him onto 'em. Driver fixed up a deal fer this feller t' come here.'

'What,' I said, 'did Strump find in them buildin's?'

Whiskers' jaw flopped down like a blacksmith's apron. The funniest look come over his face. Then he hauled up his lip and give me a stare that was smooth as a millstone. 'I never ast him,' he said, and shut his mouth.

'Didn't he never say?'

'No,' Whiskers said mighty short and, getting into his galluses, went over and made a lot of noise with the stove.

I said, 'What'd you find over there when you looked?'

'Who says I looked!'

'Get a lantern,' I said. 'We'll go over there with you.'

He didn't like it. He started to splutter, then he went off and got himself into more clothes.

'You're jest wastin' your time,' he growled when he come back and joined us with a lighted lantern. 'They ain't nobody buried no loot around here.'

It seemed colder than ever outside in that snow after the smelly warmth inside the saloon. I wondered who had made them tracks on the porch and I wondered how bad he was lying about Strump.

There wasn't nothing much to be seen in the first shack. It wasn't nothing but a ramshackle shell with the glass broke out and the rooftree sagging like it would go any minute. There wasn't no floor but the naked earth with a tatter of old papers lying round amongst it.

'Who done all the diggin'?' I said, pointing round.

The old man shrugged. He wouldn't meet my eye.

'Did you give Strump a shovel?'

'I give him the loan of one, but I told him the same thing I jest told you. There ain't no one never buried nothin' round here. This was old Burt Hunt's place. He were pore as a church mouse.'

The other shack was bigger by one extry room. There was paint on the walls that had been a bright red. There was part of a glass in one of the windows and the roof still was able to keep out the weather. It had a wood floor but a lot of the boards had been took off and someone had pawed up the ground underneath it. 'Catawamp Annie's,' Whiskers said sourly, 'an' don't ast me who the hell pried them boards off.'

152

'Never would of guessed Strump could be such a gopher. "Gopher" Strump,' Moran said, and laughed nasty.

I said, 'It wouldn't of been young Dandy, would it?'

Whiskers glared, disgusted. 'Do you think that dude would dirty his paws? About all he done was set round an' deal cards. He talked me into one two-handed stud game but he were too slick fer me an' I damn quick knowed it. Then he talked hoss. He et in my place an' the night he stayed he slep' there likewise. He went fer two-three rides of a mornin' on his paint. He changed his duds a couple times. Aside from that he wasn't outa my sight the whole time he was up here.'

I said, 'What do you suppose has happened to Strump's mother?'

'Strump's mother?' Whiskers' mouth fell open and he stared at us blank like.

'She ain't out to their place,' Moran said. 'There ain't no one.'

'Dude has prob'ly took her over to the Bluffs'. Him an' that girl's goin' t' git—Hell's fire! I plumb fergot! That girl's disappeared—the kid come by here a while ago huntin' her!'

CHAPTER SEVENTEEN

We struck out for Rafter's camp on the double. That was where old Whiskers claimed the kid had took off for and we sure didn't have no time to be wasting. If Strump ever got to that kid before I did—

I didn't cotton to be looking over them kind of thoughts.

The moon was up. It made the snow gleam like a frosted window. Far away, as we dropped down out of the mountains, we could see the winking lights of Greenback. It wasn't so cold when we got off the benches. Our broncs made a sound like they was galloping on cardboard, I noticed these things but my mind wasn't on them. Deep down inside me I was sick with fear.

I'd found out how mistaken a feller could be. I had seen how easy you could read things wrong, things that in themselves might be the absolute truth yet could look a heap different according to how you seen them. I was scared to hell I might of guessed wrong someplace.

Moran had been all for going back to Strump's but I was betting my stack Strump wouldn't be there and I was too on edge to be setting round idle when so many damn things was hung in the balance. A wrong guess now could play hell with this country.

I should of gone out to Bluff's ranch direct from town. I could see that now. It might of made no difference but I ought to of done it. It was plain as a camel would of been in this snow that they was moving Bluff's cattle into Hack Sloan's basin. If Drumm had set men to watching them west side passes they might hold Driver back for a while, but I wasn't risking nothing they would hold him back long. Any feller slick as Driver would expect opposition. If he was half as cagey as I had him figured he'd of laid some pipe in advance to beat it. Whatever else he was, Driver wasn't no fool.

We come down off the benches. We swept into the basin going hellity larrup. No sparing of horse-flesh now—no time for it. Time was a wild thing racing against us, a treacherous thing with Death in the saddle and Hell for its quirt. A clatter of rifle sound slammed from the passes and Moran pulled up with a ripped-out curse.

'Hold it, you fool!' I said. 'Them ain't your cattle!'

'Don't you reckon I know that? They're Bluff's!' Moran snarled. 'It's that ~~goddam~~ Driver! He's—'

'You said Drumm had men in them passes to stop him.'

'They ain't stop—'

He let it go with a curse. We set there tense and stiff in the cold and heard what I'd

155

thought to be hearing sooner, gunfire chattering out of the south, out of that country where Drumm was camped, out of the place where he'd bedded his cattle. In a ragged tatter of up-and-down sound rifles took up their chanting like coyotes barking and Moran ripped out a gusty oath. He flung himself down on his horse like a plaster and away we tore in the light of the stars in a madman's race across the gleaming snow.

It was Strump, I reckoned. I had looked for him to do it. He was hitting that trail herd of Rafter cattle, trying to scatter them from hell to breakfast in a play geared to cover Tom Driver's advance with the Straddle Bug beef into Rattlesnake Basin. He played for greater stakes than two hundred steers and had sold Drumm out for what he looked to gain when Driver's crew held this country at gun-point. Drumm had all the time knowed Jude Strump for a Judas and there wasn't no reason he should of been caught napping. Maybe he had looked for this snow to stop Strump, but Strump couldn't stop—he was in too deep. He daren't stop now; he had burned his bridges.

Gun sound rose in a flurry of fury and fell away in a futile popping that told of a terrified herd stampeding. Strump would pull clear now. His purpose accomplished, Jude Strump and his crew would scatter for cover.

I was betting they had.

There was no more firing, and when we

come in sight of Sloan's buildings they was frosted mounds in a frozen quiet. Leafless stems of the naked cottonwoods ran black shadows across a white blanket that was tore in the middle where several shod horses had cut through the yard going south in a hurry. Strump's bunch, I guessed, on their way to hit Rafter.

I wondered if the kid had reached Drumm's camp or if Jude Strump had cut him off from it. With a kind of black dread my thoughts touched Lovelee and sheered away from her.

We come into Sloan's yard in the tracks of Strump's riders.

Moran wasn't whistling *Red Wing* now. Moran was swearing, soft and bitter. The crack of a rifle bit sharp through it. Something belted my shoulder. I seen the ground coming. The quiet crashed into a million pieces and pain beat through me in blinding waves. I was plowing the snow with my face for a shovel. With the way that damned horse kept jerking me round I never could afterwards see how I done it, but I managed someway to keep hold of the reins. It was a thing I had learned at the Hashknife, that a man left afoot ain't worth a plugged peso. The rifle kept banging and, someplace close by, a six-shooter answered its barks with more racket, and all that while I could hear Moran cursing.

CHAPTER EIGHTEEN

The echoes quit banging their sound off the buildings and, off in some faraway part of the world, I could hear the faint flutter of hoofs going north.

Moran dug himself up out of the snow and the next thing I seen we was in Sloan's house with a lamp in my face and Moran's knife in my shoulder. For a second I thought I was going to go crazy and then, for a while, I didn't think nothing. When I come to again he had me all bandaged up and was wiping his hands on the slack of his shirttail. He said, 'You never missed hell by more than a whisper.'

I scowled, trying to make out his face through the lamp glare. I tried to get up and great splinters of pain raveled out of my shoulder. 'Lay still, you idjit,' Moran growled.

'What the hell happened?'

'We run into a ambush,' Moran spat, disgusted. 'There was only one of 'em—Strump, I reckon.'

He moved the lamp to a table.

I seen the dead rats.

Moran stuffed his shirt in. He cursed Jude Strump, cursed his luck and the weather. 'We're out of it now. You're due fer a bed an—'

'Bed, hell!' I said. 'Get me off this sofa.'

He folded his arms and backed off and

glared at me. In the light of the lamp he looked old and bitter.

The wind made a sound like six below and every damn timber in Sloan's house groaned.

I groaned, too, but I got up off the sofa.

The room whirled round like someone had kicked it. I didn't feel warm but there was sweat all over me. I waited till the room swung back into focus and I could see Moran once instead of six of him. 'Where's my horse at?'

'You fool! Git back on that bed!'

'Help me on with this coat,' I said, gritting my teeth.

Moran backed away from me. 'You can't go out with a shoulder like that, Dan—you wantin' t' kill yourself?' He got in front of the doorway, blocking it. 'You stay here. I'll send the boys after you— Hell, you can't go noways! We only got one horse!'

'One's all I need.'

I got myself into that coat and buttoned it. I seen my hat on the floor. I come pretty nigh joining it. I finally had to get down and sneak up on it. I crouched on my knees and one hand, shaking. I grabbed up the hat and sloshed it on and pulled myself back onto my feet.

Moran's eyes stuck out like knobs on a stick. I started for the back door and reached it and opened it. It was just like a draft from the mouth of the Yukon. I gritted my teeth and stumbled out.

Moran come after me, swearing a blue

streak. 'You can't hev that horse! I got t' git down an' tell Drumm about Driver.'

'I'll tell Drumm,' I said, and didn't slow down none. Wind come round the house corners, shrieking. It was pretty rough going but I made out to get myself to the horse.

'Give me a hand up into that saddle.'

Moran didn't like it but he done it anyway. He looked up at me sullen. 'We sure can't make no time ridin' double.'

'We ain't ridin' double,' I said. 'So long.'

And before he could snatch at the bridle I'd left him.

*　　　*　　　*

It was crowding three when I found Drumm's outfit. I hadn't rightly figured on cutting their sign. I'd been angling around trying to raise Gun Creek, figuring to crosscut south of the basin and make direct up the Tonto to Bluff's. I'd gone about six miles when I come down off a ridge and rode right into them. Their tongues wasn't feeling none frolicsome and their looks was colder than a bartender's heart. The loss of that herd and the work it had made them hadn't put them in no mood to be polite to no Ranger.

'Where's Drumm?' I said, breaking up the silence.

The straw boss shifted his cud and spat. 'Ain't he been with you?'

I got it then. It come over me then like the side of a mountain.

Drumm had been so sure. He hadn't made no bones about blaming the Bluffs. Drumm with his soft drawling voice and his charity. Drumm who had looked at the ground and plumb earnest had told me how a Bluff had killed Varlance. It was Drumm that had told me them boots was young Dandy's, Drumm that had give me that dope about Driver.

I stared out over the hoof-tracked snow and heard him tell of that shriveled pie and the two shriveled rats he had seen beside it, and I dug my bronc so hard with the hooks he like to of run plumb out from under me.

It wasn't much over ten mile to Bluff's ranch and I got there just as the night was fading into the cold bleak gray before dawn.

I crossed the plank bridge reading sign of two riders, two who had come this way pretty recent. My pulses quickened. The pain of my shoulder was almost forgotten as my heart leaped with hope. 'Please God,' I muttered, 'let one of 'em be Lovelee.'

I turned into the yard.

There was no saddled horses standing any place in sight though I pretty soon found where three of them had stood. Tracks went from them to the door of the house and, in one of these sets, plainer tracks come back.

Something gleamed half hid in the snow by the porch.

I pretty near fell trying to get out of the saddle. My bullet-bored shoulder set up a fresh howling, but I drove myself to that half-seen shining. The snow in the lee of the porch wasn't deep, hardly more than two inches. I bent over the gleam and come up with a six-gun, a shortbarreled Colt that I knew was Lovelee's. Her initials was on it, carved pretty in the grip.

I looked at the house with the gun in my hand while memory fetched up its kaleidoscope pictures. I crossed the porch with dragging steps and put a gloved hand on the knob of the door. I did not knock. I did not call out. A man don't expect the dead to answer.

There was a empty, all-gone feeling inside me as I twisted the knob and pulled open the door.

Jude Strump had played with a stacked deck, and lost.

CHAPTER NINETEEN

The killer's hand had been forced again.

That's the trouble about killing, someone always gets wise to it. You can't just down a guy and then call it quits. You got to keep right on to get shut of the first job. You got to keep on if you want to keep living—you got to keep on till the blood of it drowns you.

I had seen this coming—Strump's death, I mean. He had asked for it too plain. Much too plain, though I'd hoped to prevent it. But a guy can't be in more than one place at once and, since I'd woke up, both the killer and Strump had kept out of my reach.

I had never agreed with Moran's conclusion that Strump was the killer. Moran had jumped to that notion on account of the clothes we had found in Strump's feed bin. There was only one thing about them clothes that told anything—the unwashed blood of Harry Bluff that was on them. There wasn't nothing on them to tell who had worn them; they was cheap, common duds like most fellers wears. All you could tell was they'd got blood on them, which had made it seem smart for the killer to be rid of them. It had likewise looked smart to be rid of Jim's boots.

It would of been a heap smarter to of done with them things what the killer had done with the two first bodies.

Jude Strump had give me the answer to that. Strump with his poking round and his digging. No feud had forged this chain of murder. Lust for power had foaled this horror and desire for security had surely sired it. I should of guessed what was up the first time the killer and me had swapped looks. I should of seen the plain truth when it was right there before me. Some had seen parts and had paid for their knowledge, but Bluff had been doomed from the very start, and the start of this business was five weeks back, the day Hack Sloan had left Drumm in the basin. Bluff had stayed in the quick by not being round. When he'd come back from Willcox he had died in a hurry.

*   *   *

The sun was just rolling over the mountains when a third borrowed bronc brought me back to Strump's buildings. There wasn't no sounds disturbing the stillness, but hid from the place by forty rods and some cedars was Drumm's saddled gelding standing spent on spread legs. He was ringing wet and still heaving. He never knowed when I passed him. He never knowed I was round.

I lifted the gun from my unbuttoned holster. I shook out its shells and replaced them with cartridges taken fresh from my belt. When a man wants to fire he wants to fire in a hurry. With the gun in my fist I moved toward the barn, toward the little side door that hung jammed and open on one bent hinge.

No sound broke the hush of that empty yard. I felt a dry kind of tightness closing in on my throat and I was colder right then in that sunshiny brightness than I'd been last night when I was lost in the blizzard. I knowed I ought to been shamed, a growed man like me,

164

to admit his knees could be shaking like mine was.

An old wagon wheel, rim and spokes rimmed with snow, leaned against the side of the barn near the door. I looked at the icicles shining from the eaves, at the snow-covered poles of the empty corrals and the snow-crowned roofs of the huddled buildings, and wished to hell I'd never heard of the Rangers.

I looked again across the glintering snow of that yard and didn't like it no better. Where was Strump's horses? Where was his hands? Why was the place so still?

I got off my horse and looked round again. I looked at the gun in my fist and shivered. I flexed my fingers and took a couple cautious steps. My boots crunched through that frozen quiet like hell and forty acres emigrating on cart wheels.

I grabbed a long breath that was more than half sob and followed Drumm's tracks to the barn and stood listening. I couldn't hear so much as the twitter of a bird, but I smelt what I thought to smell—lavender perfume.

Lavender perfume.

Lovelee's choice. That much I knew.

I guess I prayed.

I stepped inside.

Scrinching my back flat against a wall, with the outside glare still making red spots in front of my eyeballs, I stretched my ears for the least shred of sound.

There must of been some but I didn't hear it.

Not even so much as a breath disturbed me.

I was shifting my weight when a Texas voice said out of the black: 'You suspicioned me right from the start, I reckon.'

I couldn't talk. I couldn't swallow. I was a man with life but without power of movement. All the while I'd been getting up the guts to come in here and find what my eyes had been afraid they would find, he'd been setting here watching me, grinning and chuckling.

I reckoned his gun was about a inch from my body, but all of a sudden I didn't care. I forgot my own gun. I forgot I was scared. I was crouching to jump him when my eyes got to working and I seen, plumb surprised, there wasn't nobody there.

One box stall stood empty before me, strong with horse smell, manure and hay. To my right was the glare of the open door. At my left sacked feeds and fertilizer cut off my view of the rest of the floor space. I was fixing to round them when Lovelee said, 'I suppose that's the knife you used to kill Dad with.'

'You suppose correct,' said the Texas drawl. 'I've got the blood honed off. You'll find it's nice an' sharp now.'

I couldn't stand there no longer. They was over me someplace up in that loft and every nerve in me itched to get up there.

I come away from the wall, setting down my

feet careful, picking my way through the dark spots and sunbars, easing myself around the sacked feeds and fertilizer and praying like hell there wouldn't none of them planks creak. I had to watch my footing not to knock nothing over, and that was the way I come up to the ladder.

That blood-curdling devil was still orating.

I took a deep breath. I grabbed a rung and looked upwards.

Drumm was above me peering into the loft. There was a gun in his fist and he looked fixing to use it.

He must of felt the pull of my weight on the ladder.

He looked down and seen me. He started to move. The ladder screaked like a rusty gate hinge.

'Watch out!' Lovelee screamed, and a bullet's explosion clouted the rafters and smashed like an axe against inch planking. Drumm flailed the air with his arms and fell backward. Shrunk against the ladder I crouched there rooted and stared straight into the killer's eyes.

This was the end. I guess the both of us knowed it. 'Joe,' I said, 'I—'

We must of both fired together. The whole barn shook. The kid come out of the loft head first and struck the floor like a sack of corn. I didn't look down. I went on up the ladder and cut Strump's mother and Lovelee loose. My hands shook so bad when I come to Lovelee. I thought I never should get her free and, afterwards— Well, she was kind of worked up like. I reckoned that accounted for what Drumm seen when he come back from helping Mrs. Strump to the house.

*   *   *

Drumm said, 'I would of shot him myself if I hadn't fell off that ladder.' He looked at Lovelee with a sheepish grin. 'When I remembered them rats I knowed it couldn't of been you, ma'am. I knowed a nice girl like you wouldn't poison no pie for old Hack Sloan to feed his hungry self on. It jest had t' be Dandy—'

'But that's not Dandy!' Lovelee cried. She wriggled out of my arms. 'Tell him, Dan.'

I wasn't feeling too proud about the way I had handled this chore Burt had give me. Any feller with sense would of grabbed that kid right off at the start and never got sidetracked like the way I had been.

I said, 'That feller's Joe Finch—wanted over in Texas for murder an' robbery an' a whole heap of other things. I thought it was Finch the first time I clapped eyes to him only I didn't rightly see how it could be. Driver said Dandy hadn't never been nowhere, and he hadn't of course, but I wasn't takin' Driver's word for it. I done a little askin' round on my own hook

168

but all the answers I got was the same; Dandy hadn't never been out of the Tonto. Where I went haywire was in thinking of Joe Finch as Harry Bluff's son—an' your brother,' I said to Lovelee.

'I tried to tell you—'

'Sure. I can see you did. I woke up, too, but by the time I did Mister Finch was keepin' himself out of my way. I couldn't tell no one else.'

'You coulda told me,' Drumm said, looking peeved.

'Maybe I could, but suppose I'd been wrong? Suppose you had gunned him and he really was Dandy? I hadn't no proof. All I had was a pile of thought an' some guesswork. I didn't have enough to arrest him on, even. He'd of laughed in my face.'

'How'd you get onto him?'

'Well, you helped some. But mostly it was little things, things that didn't tie right. Dandy, judgin' by what I could pick up, had been a quiet-natured feller mostly interested in horses. Never drunk, swore, or smoked. Never fiddled with the pasteboards. It looked like he'd done a heap of changin' lately. He'd been slippin' down to Widney's, playin' cards an' drinking'. He seemed quarelsome an' broody, an' he looked so much like Finch I could taste it.

'No two guys, I told myself, could ever in this world look that much alike. He just plain *had* to be Finch. Only if Finch wasn't Dandy, it looked like Harry Bluff would of mighty quick seen it. When I thought about that things begun to line up for me.

'I had heard about Dandy goin' up to Gisela, about him waitin' round for a guy that never showed. I'd heard of old Bluff goin' off down to Willcox. When I found out Bluff had only got back that night—the night he was killed—I seen pretty quick the kid was probably Finch an' not Dandy at all. The kid hadn't been with Bluff hardly no time on the ride to Roblero's when he got the bright notion of hunting that horse. Then a few minutes later Harry Bluff quit the bunch. It all doved in once I knowed what to look for. Sloan, Trumbet, Strump, an' Tom Driver all fit in snug once I'd made up my mind that the kid was Finch.

'It's a cinch Driver started it. Driver knew Finch looked a lot like the kid; he knew all about Joe Finch from the Rangers. He knowed Finch needed a place to hole up. He didn't have to sweat none about Bluff's crew, he could hold them in line an' they would keep their mouths shut; Driver knew how to handle driftin' gun stiffs. What he wanted was power, an' he seen how to get it if Finch would throw in with him. There wasn't no reason why Finch wouldn't fall for it. He was huntin' a hide-out an' this was a good one; he could step right into a dead man's boots. All Finch had to do was get rid of the Bluffs an' Driver and him could both have their cravings.

'So Driver got word to him. He talked Harry Bluff into goin' to Willcox and, with a yarn of fast horses, he sent Dandy to Gisela. He picked on Gisela because it was just about done for; nobody never went up there no more an' Dandy hadn't been near there inside of three years. It was just the place for a nice quiet killing. Hardly no one round to catch on to the difference when Finch come along to take Dandy's place. It was a damn slick scheme an' it come near workin'. It was the little things, really, that tripped them up.

'For one thing, Finch's talk. Finch's talk was spiced with Texas, like Driver's. Old Man Bluff had come from Kentucky an' Dandy hadn't never been out of the Tonto. Finch was wise to this an' mostly he managed to keep his mouth shut. I had noticed his Texas talk right away an' had several times wondered why he talked so little—about the only time he ever opened his mouth was when somethin' riled him so damn bad he had to. Lovelee done most of the talkin' for them an' both Finch an' Driver watched her like hawks. They took mighty good care to keep her in hearin'.'

Drumm scratched at his jaw. 'How about Sloan—he wasn't in with them, was he?'

'No,' I said. 'Sloan come into it right after Dandy. He'd gone up to Gisela that day for supplies—remember you told me? The

171

bartender up there says he never seen Hack. I figure Sloan must of stumbled onto Finch an' Dandy together. Mebbe he seen the actual killin'. He seen enough, anyway, that Finch had to kill him. When we find the one I think we'll find the other; I think Finch dug one hole for both of them.'

'But what about Lovelee?' I seen Drumm look at her, puzzled. 'Looks like she could of found some way to of tipped you off. Didn't she never suspect—'

'Of course she did,' I said. 'She was scairt half to death an' I knowed she was. She tried several times to get it across to me, but each time Finch or Driver cut her off. They stuck to her closer than flies round a honey dip, an' when you give me that sign-readin' lecture at Sloan's I jumped to the notion that was what had scared her. The only time I got to see her alone—she had slipped off from Driver while Finch was off tryin' to gun Les Trumbet—'

'Trumbet!' growled Drumm, 'Did that skunk kill Trumbet?'

I nodded. 'We'll prob'ly never know what Trumbet seen, but I think he seen Finch with a shovel in his hand. Soon as Finch found out he'd been up to Gisela—an' he found out from Strump who was tryin' to swap silence for cash and other valuable considerations—Trumbet's hours was numbered.

'But, like I was startin' to say, the only time Lovelee had a real chance to tell me what was

172

going on, my temper an' her pride kind of got in the way. It wasn't till two–three hours afterwards that I finally tumbled to the way things stood an' realized Finch was Finch an' not Dandy.'

'Excusin' me, ma'am,' Drumm said, kind of fussed, 'but why in the devil didn't Finch kill *you*?'

'She's a girl,' I said, 'an' a mighty fine one. Finch had other plans for her if he could find some way to keep her mouth shut. It was another of them things Driver hadn't counted on.'

'Well,' Drumm said, pulling on his gloves, 'I'll go round up the boys an' we'll take care of Driver. If it's land that he's wantin' I'll see that he gits some he kin hev forever.'

I tried in my stumbling way to cheer Lovelee. I said, 'It's all over now.'

'An' you'll be goin' away.'

'I might come back sometime.'

She fiddled with a fold in her skirt real intent like. 'I ain't never been much in favor of—you know—of waitin',' she said.

I seen her look at me slanchways. 'If you wasn't so set on bein' a Ranger—if you had any mind to run a ranching business—Well! can't you never say *anything*?'

I not only could—I did. And I done it the way talk listens best to women—with gestures.